MW01518205

Into the Snow

The Testimony and Last Will

of

Jedediah P. Carpenter

John Erwin

This story is for
the
spirits of the Sprucetree

and

for
Christine, Teri, Ben, and Bob,
without whose support
and encouragement
it would not have been written.

Mount Silverheels dominates the landscape in the northern end of South Park, a rolling prairie ringed by high mountains in central Colorado. Rising to an elevation of 13,822 feet above sea level, Mount Silverheels overlooks the headwaters of the Middle Fork of the South Platte River and the mining camps of Buckskin Joe, Alma, Montgomery, Fairplay, and Como.

It is named in memory of a dance-hall girl . . .

LAST WILL AND TESTAMENT

I, Jedediah P. Carpenter, declaring myself to be of sound mind, do herein set forth my Last Will and Testament, dated this sixteenth day of December in the Year of Our Lord 1916, in what remains of the town of Buckskin Joe, Park County, Colorado (formerly Jefferson Territory, even if the powers that be, residing east of the Mississippi, never formally recognized it as such).

Two hours ago I called upon God Almighty as my witness, but He hasn't shown Himself yet; and, there being no other human beings within a day's slog through hip-deep snow, I call instead as my witnesses to this document the following: the bitter wind howling down from the pass prying its icy fingers through the cracks between the logs I have neglected to chink these past decades; the heat waves rising from the wood stove with its belly full of glowing spruce embers; and the cry of the lynx I heard near the timber's edge this morning before daybreak. I have few worldly goods to leave behind, so I am confident the veracity of these witnesses will not be questioned.

I hereby leave all of my possessions to the living descendants of Emma Cooper, if any can be found. I believe there was a daughter born to her in St. Louis sometime in 1859 or 1860, not my child, alas, but dear to me nonetheless, if she did, indeed, survive into a fruitful adulthood. I suppose there could be children or grandchildren, or even great-grandchildren by now, with names and whereabouts unknown to me.

In any case, my meager belongings are theirs, to be divided equally among them, and if such living descendants cannot be found, then it is my wish that all of my property be given to the people of Park County, to be used in whatever manner may benefit the populace at large.

The following list includes most of my possessions and property, but everything I own is to be included in this Will even if I fail to specifically mention it here:

This cabin, on the sunny side of the gulch above Buckskin Creek, which I built with my own hands in the fall of 1859, houses everything I own (except the tools in the shed out back and the four cords of firewood stacked at the edge of the meadow beyond the shed).

Now, my conscience demands a confession: I may not actually own this cabin and the property it sits upon. I lost it to Red of the auburn hair and crooked nose from Indiana (never caught his real name) at about two in the morning late in the spring of 1863, I believe it was, in the days before I had the good sense to avoid drawing to an inside straight. I signed my deed over to him, but the Mendosas ambushed him on the road to Fairplay before he could record the transfer. I've been waiting all these years for some of his kin to appear to claim his property (including the deed which I removed from inside his boot before we hauled him off to the undertaker), but they have never shown up, so I suppose I still hold legal claim to the place, even if morally and ethically it may belong to someone else.

The rest of the things are mine free and clear. Like I said before, it doesn't amount to much. The Sharps rifle on the rack by the door, the bow and quiver of arrows hanging from the peg below it, the cast iron pot and skillet, the blankets in the loft where I sleep. The leather mail bag behind the chimney stones contains a small pouch of gold dust, a gold pocket watch, a few questionable mining claims, and a sheaf of stock certificates I have accumulated over the years (a perseverant lawyer or accountant might be able to track the threads of ownership in those mining outfits and find those claims and certificates are worth a pretty penny; or perhaps not).

On the shelves behind the stove are all the books I own, so old and read so many times they are falling apart: a volume of Shakespeare, translations of the Greek masters, works by Darwin, Jefferson, Emerson, Channing, Lyell, and Twain, and my mother's Bible. I suppose I've had thousands of books over the years, but I gave most of them to the library down in Fairplay as I finished reading them, not wanting to burden myself with more things than I could easily load up in a wagon and move on with. Not that I really planned on ever leaving this place for more than a season or two at a stretch.

I also leave the clothes on my back, but they will be of little use after my desiccated corpse is discovered up there near timberline one of these years, so I suspect they should be left to rot along with my remains—dust to dust.

Lastly, there is a case of good Tennessee whiskey stored (hidden, actually) beneath the floor boards under the bear rug in front of the stove, but I expect most of it will be gone before I am.

So much for the Will part of this document. What remains is the Testament part, or Testimony, if you will, attached as an addendum hereto. I intend to spend a good part of this winter and on into the spring writing my story down. I've read a good many dime novels claiming to portray the days of the Old West, you know the ones you can buy from the newsstands at any of the train depots from Como to New York City—I guess travelers need something to do with their time—but I believe my story will be far more entertaining than any of those, and, unlike the works of those pretenders from back east, every word set down herein is true.

Most of what I know and have seen will not be new to anybody, but I do know a few things that might fill in some gaps here and there and solve a mystery or two. I like to think Emma Cooper 's kin might like to have these things written down, before the avalanches and vandals take out what is left of Buckskin Joe and nothing remains but the names on the maps and the epitaphs carved into the headstones out there in the Buckskin cemetery.

When I am finished with my Testimony, if the whiskey doesn't kill me first, I will secure this document beneath the aforementioned floorboards in the middle of my cabin floor and walk off into the snow. I might find I am not alone out there.

SIGNED this SIXTEENTH day of DECEMBER, 1916, in the presence of the aforementioned witnesses:

BY:

_____

Jedediah P. Carpenter

TESTIMONY

She came to me last night. Most people would say it was just a dream, but I know it was real, or even more real than real. Her raven hair shone in the moonlight as she stood there in the snow outside my front door. She beckoned me with her long slender hands to come out with her and wander among the mountains. Her face was painted like a child's doll, with ruby-red lips and a hint of rouge on her cheeks beneath her long black lashes. She smiled, but did not speak, and those gray eyes—those incredible gray eyes!—shone like fire in the night. She shook her hair back, touching her lips with her fingers and pointing up the gulch, beckoning me to join her. The snow-reflected moonlight illuminated the canyon like daylight, except for the inky black sky with millions of stars puncturing the crisp near-winter air.

I held the door open wide and responded to her gestures, "Hang on, Emma, let me get my coat and boots." I grabbed my coat from the peg and pulled my boots on, then stepped down into the snow to follow her. But she was gone. There were no tracks in the snow and I found myself standing in cold white powder up to my knees wearing nothing but my long underwear.

It has been like this for several weeks now. The snow gets a little deeper with every passing storm and her visits come at closer intervals after five and a half decades of absence, so I know my time here is growing short. I will soon be going out into the snow to join her. So, it is time to get my story told, and in the telling to tell a little of her story, too.

"Goddam Indian." Clint Williams had said that about a thousand times since we left Fort Kearny. He said it at dawn when he got up, he said it two or three times an hour as he rode his horse beside the wagons, scanning the horizon and seeing nothing but grass and cottonwood trees, and he said it every night before he turned the watch over to one of the other scouts.

Now he said it before he bit off the end of a paper cartridge, sprinkled a little powder in the flash pan, rammed the powder and lead ball down his muzzle-loader's barrel, then extracted the ramrod, sputtering and cursing the whole time. He checked the flint, then rested the loaded weapon across the open water barrel lashed to the side of my family's wagon.

The canvas shaded us from the late morning sun as we—I say "we", but it was really me doing the digging and Clint doing the complaining—dug another shallow hole beneath the rutted trail. I threw a shovel full of dirt out of the hole and stopped to breathe. Clint eased down onto his heels and squatted in the shade beside the barrel.

"My papa never kept a loaded gun around," I said.

"That right?" Clint squinted at me from under his hat, then gazed out onto the prairie like he had forgotten I was there.

"That's right. He always said you were more likely to get killed stumbling over your own rifle than by any pack of wolves or marauding Indians. He never loaded 'til he saw his target coming. But, then, he also believed in keeping up with the latest developments in firearms, so it didn't take him as long to load his breach-loader with rim-fire cartridges as it does for you to load that old relic." Despite the gravity of my current situation, I couldn't help ribbing Clint a little about his quaint ways. He was one of the best frontier scouts I ever knew, but he had his own way of doing things, which to my young mind looked liked he was always several steps behind the rest of the world in some of the things he did.

Clint stood up and scooped a cup of water out of the barrel. He swirled a mouthful around his teeth, then spat the water out on the ground at his feet. "Well, I guess he could have seen the cholera coming from a mile off and it wouldn't have mattered whether his gun was loaded or not," he said.

I started digging again and didn't look up at Clint for a long time. When I did, he was peering over my shoulder to the south. I followed his gaze across the grass-carpeted rolling prairie. About a hundred yards away a clump of cottonwoods rose above a shallow cleft in the earth. The tallest tree was dead, standing there like a white ghost among its green companions. A couple of crows perched on a naked branch sticking out over a younger tree whose leaves rustled in a passing gust.

"Seen something out there?" I asked Clint.

"Not a damn thing," he grumbled, "but I know that red devil is out there somewheres. We been cutting his sign for days now, in every direction around us. He's a smart one, though. Never comes in close enough for us to see him or his horse or his dust."

"Maybe he's just lonesome and likes our company," I said. I threw one more load of dirt out of the hole and climbed out, using my shovel handle to push myself up. "I reckon this one's ready," I said. "I can't dig any more, anyway, so it will have to do."

"The dead can't complain," Clint said. "Let's see if that girl is finished up so we can get this over with."

We walked over to the one other wagon remaining from our wagon train, the others having fled in the midnight darkness with the first rumors of cholera on their lips—the wagon master, the scouts (all except Clint, who may have been one of the kindest men I ever knew, or maybe instead he was just too stupid for his own good) and ten families with their oxen and dogs and children, all loaded up and gone without a word to us or a backward glance.

I called out as we approached. The Cooper family's beautiful young mare—solid midnight-black except for a white blaze on its chest and a gray brand—"SC"—burned into her flank—nickered at me from where she stood hobbled a few yards away in the tall prairie grass. Emma Cooper emerged from her family's wagon and said, "They're all ready."

My mother was one of the smartest and best educated people I ever knew. I remember her talking one time about a wise old guy from way back in the past sometime who said we could never step in the same river twice, meaning, I suppose, that the world is always changing, even if in our superficial view of things it looks about the same. Most of my memories are like that. If I think too long about most events in my past, I start to realize the details are no longer clear. Sometimes I wonder if some of my memories are but memories of memories, subject to subtle changes and reinterpretations as the years roll on.

But, my memories of these particular few days are not like a river, getting caught up in rapids, then swirling out of focus in eddies and backwaters. If memories of these days are like a river, it is a river frozen solid in the dead of winter, timeless and unchanging. I have stepped in this river more times than I can count, and the images, smells and sounds are exactly the same every time: the aroma of freshly turned earth beneath broken prairie turf spoiled by the fetid stench of sickness and death, the cry of a red-tailed hawk patrolling the skies above rolling grass-covered hills, the exhaustion brought about by worry, anguish, and heartache followed by hours of hard physical labor.

I didn't cry for my parents or my baby sister, or for Emma Cooper 's family, as we laid them to rest in those shallow graves beneath the Oregon Trail. Life was hard in those years, and people died, and that was that. I was stupidly proud of myself for doing what had to be done and not showing my emotions to Clint or Emma Cooper as I worked. The crying did come, but much later.

I remember how Emma sewed the bodies up snug in wagon-canvas shrouds, and how we dug the holes right in the ruts so passing wagons would pack the ground tight and keep the wolves from digging up our loved ones' bodies and scattering their bones across the land.

I remember how dry the prairie was in the late summer of 1858 and how we camped at a buffalo wallow with stagnant pools muddied and fouled by passing travelers. I remember how my father wanted to push on for better water, but everybody was tired and just wanted to camp before the sun went down. I remember my baby sister Evie bringing me a bouquet of bright blue flowers she had picked along the trail and how she giggled and sang around the campfire and gushed about what a wonderful life we would all have together in Oregon, just a half day before she and my parents and Emma's parents got sick and then died in the most ghastly manner I can imagine, amid fevered rantings and retchings that seemed to last forever, but were mercifully short.

I've been lucky, I guess. I never got sick from the cholera or the smallpox or any other passing ailment. No bullet or knife blade aimed my direction ever hit its mark. Emma Cooper was lucky that night, too, I suppose, since the cholera didn't take her, either. At the time, though, I think we both wished we had been taken. We were too numb to cry or do anything but dig holes and sew shrouds and bury our dead.

Emma Cooper was nineteen years old and I was smitten with her. I was only sixteen and she had barely noticed me until the day our families died. Her family was from southeastern Missouri and my family just chanced to hook up with their party on our way from Arkansas up the Mississippi to St. Louis, where our wagon train was assembled for the trek west.

Emma had coal-black hair she wore in a tight bun beneath her bonnet, except in the evenings around the campfire when she would take it down and let it hang full and loose around her shoulders and down her back as she sang and danced to the fiddle music old Sawyer Jones would play. I've never heard the angels sing, but I thought she sang like one when mournful ballads or bawdy ditties rolled from her lips and she moved her body to the rhythms of the music.

My mother thought Emma was scandalous, the way she carried on for our whole camp to watch, and she often made comments about fallen women and the power they had over men the morning after one of our evening campfires. I don't recall understanding much about fallen women at that time in my life, but I am certain my curiosity was aroused. My father mostly kept silent on the subject, but I saw him watch her dance and I saw him clap his hands in time with the music on more than one night on the trail between St. Louis and that buffalo wallow in the middle of Nebraska Territory.

Emma had the most intriguing gray eyes, such as I have never seen in another woman. As a bashful and awkward sixteen-year-old, I rarely looked squarely in her direction, but when I did her eyes stood out like polished gemstones, framed by her clear white skin beneath a blue bonnet and strands of shining black hair. In later years, when we became close, I would gaze into those gray eyes and see flecks of every color dancing inside her smile. I would lose myself in her world of mystery and mischief and kindness and torment.

The evening after we buried our dead, giant thunderheads rose in the west to obscure the setting sun. I went to sleep in my sister's bedroll inside the wagon, my dreams interrupted by lightning flashes and thunder that produced no rain, but only dry gusting winds that lasted most of the night. The next morning the sky was clear blue with not a cloud in sight, from the rising sun in the east all the way to the western horizon.

"The rains will start any day now," Clint said as he wiped his plate clean with a biscuit and reached for his mug of hot tea. "I expect it will rain almost every evening until early September, once it finally gets started. We need to get this train moving, if you expect to get over South Pass before the snow flies."

"I expect so," I said. I hadn't given much thought to the future. I had a wagon loaded with my father's carpentry tools —our last name was not without meaning—and with my mother's kitchen garden seeds and garden tools, and with our personal belongings, books, and a few household goods. I also had a pair of fine oxen, hobbled on the prairie and getting fat on the thick grass.

My mother had finally gotten her way about leaving Arkansas ahead of the war clouds she saw rising all around her by convincing my father to follow my uncle's family to Oregon. She didn't know you couldn't just run from trouble and have it quietly stand aside and let you leave it behind.

We were going to Oregon to build houses for settlers and grow vegetables for their families. I don't think my folks cared anything about getting rich. They just wanted to get by, in a new land with endless possibilities. So, I guessed I would hitch up soon and keep heading west.

"I've come as far west as I ever intend to get," Emma said between bites of her biscuit. Her eyes looked tired and her face was drawn. I saw the mature woman she might become in the lines around her mouth and eyes. "I only came this far because my family gave me no choice. There is nothing but hard work and heartache west of here. I'm going back to St. Louis, or maybe even New York, or Paris, France. I want to marry a fine rich man in the east and spend the rest of my life singing and dancing in theaters in front of hundreds, or even thousands, of people."

"Your fine rich husband might object to the singing and dancing," Clint observed.

"I won't care," she said. She tossed her head and I saw a gleam of mischief in her eyes. "I will be the talk of the town and my husband will be proud to have me on his arm, or he can stay home and count his money while I find men who do appreciate me."

Well, I didn't say much, just dumbfounded to be so near such a pretty girl, and probably imagining if she ever noticed me, the real me, not the shy kid in hand-me-down trousers, that she would follow me to the ends of the earth and never even look at another man. I finished my biscuits and scrubbed out the skillet.

"Here comes trouble." Clint stood squinting to the west. I saw a trio of wagons lumbering our direction, led by a man riding a tall chestnut horse. The man wore a floppy hat I could tell, even from a hundred yards away, had once been white, but was now a soiled gray.

"That is Zeke Jones," Clint said. "He is one no-good mother's son. When he gets here, you two just let me do the talking." I made a practice of not talking much, not being very impressed with things I might have to say, especially around strangers, so I didn't mind just standing there and watching the horseman approach.

Clint hitched up his pants and felt for the knife belted in the sheath at his back. His muzzle-loader leaned against the side of Emma Cooper's wagon a good hundred feet away, not loaded. I saw Clint from time to time for twenty more years, still carrying that useless gun, when he could have had a fine revolver or breach-loading rifle with rim-fire cartridges.

Zeke Jones guided his horse uncomfortably close to our little camp before he drew up and waited for the three heavy freight wagons to come to a stop and for the ensuing dust to clear. He was a large man, wearing clothing I could have used for a tent. His boots were a good six sizes bigger than mine. He had deep-set eyes that looked black in the shadow of his hat. His face was mostly hidden by a thick black beard and scruffy hair hanging down to his eyebrows. He looked down at each of us in turn, giving Emma Cooper a longer stare than politeness called for, then spat a thin stream of tobacco juice onto the ground.

"Howdy, Clint. Looks like a fine bunch of travelers you've got yourself attached to," he said.

I observed at an early age that conversations between strangers, and sometimes conversations between long-time friends, are a lot like business transactions. Somebody usually comes out ahead at the end, even though the other party may be completely satisfied and not see the lopsided outcome. The key is to listen much and talk little. Most people like to hear themselves talk and, given the opportunity, will talk about themselves more than anything else. Sometimes, if the other person listens quietly, just injecting enough words to move things along, it is almost like the big talker forgets he is talking out loud and starts saying things he might not reveal in other circumstances. This is especially true if the conversation is lubricated with distilled spirits.

Since I am naturally shy and prefer my own company to the company of others, unless I am with a special woman or a few very close friends, it is easy for me to stay mostly quiet in social situations. By doing so, I sometimes become invisible and learn things nobody else knows.

So, I stood mute like Clint had asked us to, waiting for him to keep up our end of the conversation. He squinted up at the rider, but didn't say anything. Emma broke the silence by saying, "Good morning, Mr. Jones. My name is Emma Cooper and this boy here is Jedediah"—I cringed inwardly at her characterization of me as a 'boy'—"and I see you already know Mr. Williams. Would you and your drivers like to share some biscuits and a pot of fine English tea with us?" She was dressed in plain prairie traveling clothes, but her face radiated excitement and not-so-subtle invitation.

"Don't mind if we do, ma'am," Zeke Jones said as he dismounted. He motioned to his three drivers to do the same. They all sauntered up and squatted or took one knee near the fire. The lot of them looked mangy and disreputable.

I maneuvered myself around the fire so as to be upwind of them to the extent the prevailing wind direction could be determined. Clint passed around a basket of still-warm biscuits nestled in a checkered towel and poured tea into their waiting tin cups.

"Makin' another run east, Zeke?" Clint asked.

"Yep. The pickins have been pretty good this year. We came out by way of the Mormon Trail in June. Among more mundane items, we found a fine upright piano half way to Salt Lake. Sold it back to its original owners when we got there. I asked twice what I thought it was worth, and the wife was more than happy to come up with full payment in twenty-dollar gold pieces. Damn greenhorns, I tell 'ya." Zeke chuckled, then spat.

Clint shook his head almost imperceptibly, then asked, "Did you happen to run across a party with about ten wagons a day or two west of here?"

Zeke answered, "Yeah, we did, but I could tell there was sickness in their camp, so we steered clear and kept moving east. I might have a look at what's left there on our way back out next spring. No point in being greedy. Or impatient." He chuckled again, but this time his chuckle rolled into a deep belly laugh, followed by a phlegmy wheeze and a hack and another trickle of spit on the ground.

Clint turned to Emma and explained, "In case you haven't already caught on, Zeke here is a regular human turkey buzzard, making his living off the misfortune of others."

Zeke scowled at Clint, then leered at Emma before he said, "Me and my boys here scratch out a meager existence by collecting the unwanted and worthless cast-offs left behind by the immigrant trains. 'Waste not, want not,' my old grandma always said. I figure it's like the Law of the High Seas. Any derelict property belongs to him who can bring it home, even if the sea we traverse is grass instead of water."

I couldn't help jumping into the conversation by saying, "Well, it sounds fine to me, as long as you don't cross the line between scavenging and thievery."

Zeke looked a little surprised, as if he had never noticed I was there. "Young man, you can call God as my witness I have never laid a hand on anything that did not rightfully belong to me. If a traveler comes onto the Great American Desert fully loaded with a household's goods fit for a Boston sea captain's mansion and has to choose somewhere along the way between keeping his oxen alive or throwing his wife's favorite rocking chair over the side, well, I see nothing wrong with coming along, better equipped with stronger wagons and stronger teams, and helping myself to the bounty those pilgrims will never come back to get. And if I come upon a band of dead travelers, whether they died of thirst or cholera or at the hands of bandits or red savages, then I take no issue with taking those things said travelers will clearly not be carrying into the hereafter with them."

Clint waded in by asking, "And what about a situation where a traveler and his family may be at death's door, but they ain't quite dead yet? Who gets dibs on their possessions when you saunter up on your fine pony?"

"I'm not sure I like the direction you are taking this conversation in, Clint. You will do well to change the subject," Zeke said. He was about a foot taller than Clint and at least that much bigger around, so I didn't hold it against Clint one bit when he backed down and quietly stirred the embers in the fire pit.

"Now take you people here, for instance." Zeke glanced at me and fixed his gaze on Emma, his eyes coming to rest a little below the neckline of her frock. "I see the two of you and I see four oxen and two wagons. I suspect if I poked around in those piles of fresh dirt I would find your families. Now, do you expect to keep going west, or are you ready to consider a generous offer for the purchase of your outfits, along with our fine companionship on the road back to the mighty Mississippi? For example, young lady, that mare over yonder grazing beyond your wagon is a fine piece of horse-flesh. She would command a pretty penny anywhere between

New York and San Francisco. I wouldn't mind giving you twice what she is worth and keeping her for myself."

"We haven't decided yet," I said, before Emma had a chance to answer.

She glared at me and mouthed a question, "WE??" with upturned eyebrows indicating her opinion that the concept was ridiculous. Then she turned to Zeke and said, "No, we don't know yet. I might say, though, the prospect of heading west into the high country with snow coming on does not thrill me one bit. Maybe if you make the right kind of offer, we will have something to think about."

Zeke finished his breakfast and motioned for his companions to return to their wagons. "I tell you what, young lady, and young gentleman (nodding towards me, but still staring at her), we are going to head east about a mile, make a dry camp away from this stinking water hole and rest for a day or two. Y'all just come on over if you want to talk specifics." He touched the brim of his hat, mounted his horse and led his caravan away.

They were out of earshot and their dust had blown to the south before Clint leaned back on his elbows and addressed Emma Cooper. "'Young lady and young gentleman', my right eye. Don't you get snared by Zeke Jones and his frontier charm. His charm is like the charm of a rattlesnake. He will mesmerize you with those coal-black eyes and then strike before you see what's coming. Girl, I don't know much about you, but I know you are all alone out here. It ain't really my business, but you can do a whole lot better than cast your lot with Zeke Jones and his crowd. He will promise you money you will never see, as he takes you and all of your things away from here where there are no witnesses. God only knows what might happen to you then."

Emma laughed a little, then said, "I think I know how to handle men, Mr. Williams. And you are right—it's not your business what I decide to do. But, I thank you for caring." Then she turned to me and said, "And don't you think about you and me in the same breath, Buster. There ain't no "we" in this camp. I make my own choices. Understand?"

I'm sure my face turned beet red and I might have even teared up some, from a little embarrassment and a whole lot of anger, as I said, "Yes, ma'am. I wouldn't presume to ever tell you what to do."

We spent another night there, with another round of thunderheads and lightning and dry wind keeping us company until dawn. After more biscuits and tea—Clint carried a big block of tea in his saddlebags and whittled off a chunk to brew up a pot every chance he got—Emma Cooper asked me to help her hitch up her team. She was heading east to dicker with Zeke Jones, and to go back to St. Louis on her own if she didn't like the terms he offered.

"You could stay with me," I said. "I don't know what lies ahead for me, but I swear to you I would keep you safe, whatever we end up doing." I made this offer in a spirit of generosity roused by genuine concern for her well-being, along with a large helping of foolishness brought on by being sixteen years old and drunk with an ill-defined longing at being in her presence.

She smiled, a gentle, genuine smile that touched me to the depths of my soul, then she shook her head and said, "I know you would try to keep me safe, Jedediah P. Carpenter, but you have no idea what you are asking. There is nothing west of here I want, and I would be nothing but a misery to you."

So I helped her get her outfit together. Then I walked beside her wagon to Zeke's camp. I stood off a ways watching a hawk gliding over the grass until it snatched a mouse, then she came back to me and said, "I made a deal. I'm heading to St. Louis with Zeke, and maybe to New Orleans. I wish you the best of fortune, Jed," and she held out her hand and we shook. That was the first time I ever touched a girl who was not my nearest kin. Her touch sent an electric shock through me that swirled around in my head and made my heart dance with joy, and with possibility. I will never forget that touch, even beyond the grave.

She headed east, driving her team with an easy touch showing rare skill for anyone, much less a woman. Her horse, "Star of Midnight" she called her, followed along behind her wagon with a long tether around her neck securely tied to the hinge of the back gate. Zeke's three freight wagons followed behind for a spell, then fanned out to both sides of her to avoid the thick dust rising from her wagon's wheels and her oxen's feet. Zeke stood beside his horse and gazed out across the prairie, then he spat into a clump of prickly pears and watched the procession for a few minutes before he mounted up to ride.

I called out to him before he moved out. "Mr. Jones!" I said, then I marched up to look at him sitting on his horse.

"Got somethin' to say to me, boy?" he asked.

"I do, sir," I said. "I hope you have only the most honest mercantile interest in that girl's property. I hope you intend to deliver her safely to St. Louis with your money safely tucked away in her purse. But I tell you right now if I ever find out you treated her badly in any way, I will hunt you down and do things to you that will make you wish you were dead."

My knees trembled as I made this proclamation, and I hope to this day my voice was not shaking along with them, but I said what I had to say and that was that.

Zeke Jones leaned his head back and roared with laughter. Then he cast me a cold glance and said, "You sniveling little runt. Keep talking big like that and you might run across somebody who doesn't take it kindly. Now, run along and mind your own damn business."

He spat again, nearly hitting my boots with a stream of sweet-stinking brown tobacco juice, then rode away to catch up with his party.

The next morning Clint Williams and I hitched up my oxen and we headed west. We were just a few dozen miles east of the confluence of the South Platte and North Platte rivers. We planned to stop there for a few days to hunt and relax and let his horse and my oxen graze on the healthy grass fed by the rivers' constant moisture.

Towards afternoon we met an eastbound rider, who veered our direction and started waving his hat and yelling. As he drew near, I could make out his words.

"GOLD!" he hollered. "William Green Russell's party has discovered GOLD ON CHERRY CREEK!"

He pulled up in front of us, breathing and blowing almost as hard as his horse. "I've seen it myself," he gasped. "Gold by the bucketful right there for the taking!"

"Slow down and breathe, mister," Clint told him. "Let's make camp right here. You can join us for some beans and cornbread and tell us all about it."

So we made camp. The excited traveler said folks called him Shorty—when he got down from his horse I noticed he was not an inch under six feet five—so we introduced ourselves. Clint built a fire from prairie grass and dry buffalo chips and proceeded to heat beans in a pot and to bake cornbread in my cast iron Dutch oven.

When we sat to eat, Clint told Shorty to tell us all about the gold on Cherry Creek.

"I've been trapping and trading all along the mountain front for thirty years," he said, "and I would wager I've camped at the mouth of Cherry Creek where it runs into the South Platte and tramped all over that country a dozen times and never had the slightest idea I was that close to gold! William Green Russell and his men and a few Cherokees from Georgia spent a good deal of this summer prospecting. They found good color on what they're calling Little Dry Creek, and made a fine strike on Cherry Creek. Word is getting out. I bet this time next year that area will be crawling with prospectors. I'm heading back to St. Louis to put an outfit together—picks and shovels and pans and so forth—and I'll be back out here before the snow melts, I can tell you that."

Well, this news had a mesmerizing effect on Clint Williams. He and Shorty stayed up long into the night going over every detail Shorty could recall about Cherry Creek and the Pikes Peak country. I had a feeling my scout and only remaining companion would be leaving the next day, not going where I intended to go, which was Oregon. I couldn't blame him, really. The lure of easy riches is enticing to any man, no matter what he may be doing or how happy the life he is leading may be. But, I had other plans. I had an aunt and uncle who had gone to Oregon a few years before and I expected to join up with them to create something worthwhile and lasting on the western edge of the continent. So, I determined to keep going west on the Oregon Trail even if Clint decided otherwise.

Clint sidled up to me before we turned in for the night and said, "Jed, this may be my best chance to make some real money before I get too old to ride a horse. I would feel really bad about going back to St. Louis without you, so how's about you and me join up and go back together? We could put a prospecting outfit together in no time and head back out before the crowds show up."

"Thanks for asking, Clint," I said, "but my uncle and aunt are expecting me in Oregon. Don't worry about leaving me here. I can take care of myself."

The next morning, Clint and Shorty took off together for St. Louis to hole up for the winter and to gear up for a season of prospecting. They both figured to put in six or eight months of staking claims and scooping nuggets out of creeks, then retire back east as rich gentlemen of great importance. Clint was a fine scout and had been working the Oregon Trail and Mormon Trail for ten years or more, so I wondered how he would adjust to his planned life of leisure. But, I was young and didn't know much then and wished him well when he told me of his plans.

He did make one more wide sweep around our camp before he left, riding in a circle taking in all of the prairie within a half mile of my wagon. When he rode back up, I saw the worry on his face. "That goddam Indian is still sniffing around," he said. "I'll be danged if he didn't camp within a mile or two of here just last night. I'm half inclined to stick around a while and see you safe to South Pass or even farther."

"Don't worry about me, Clint," I said. "I will be fine." The truth is, I was not confident about moving west alone, but at the same time, I thought being alone was exactly what I needed. I really wasn't too worried about the Indian, if there really was one following us—Clint was a good scout and had become a good friend, but he did have a larger imagination than most. The few Indians we had encountered since we left

St. Louis had been friendly and mostly minding their own business, so I didn't think I was in any real danger. I knew from listening to other scouts and travelers that far more people died trying to cross rivers along the trail than had ever been murdered by marauding Indians.

I looked back a few times into the east as I led my wagon west, watching until I could not see Clint's dust lingering on the horizon any longer. Occasional hot gusty winds blew out of the northwest. I smelled dust and the musky smell of fresh buffalo manure and the smoke from faraway fires. The light had made the subtle shift from high mid-summer brightness to the lowering shades of oncoming autumn.

When people think of the Oregon Trail, I expect most of them envision a single tidy path the width of a wagon's axle leading from St. Louis all the way to the Pacific. But that is not the way it was. The trail did narrow down to a single pair of ruts when the land forced travelers through narrow canyons or other tight places, but for most of its route, the "trail" was an ill-defined expanse of beaten-down grass and widely spaced ruts where families had tried to pick the best route from water hole to river to creek based on their own dead reckoning or instinct or the advice of scouts, or places where trains of a hundred wagons would fan out across the prairie to avoid eating each other's dust as they rolled through rainless summers and miles of unchanging landscape.

My first day alone on the prairie I picked a faded trail trending a little south of west heading toward a line of cottonwoods far out near the horizon. Cottonwood trees often mean water, and I was concerned about setting out much further west without refilling my water barrels. I thought finding a flowing creek would be a good idea.

One thing I noticed as my family moved west, leaving the wooded Mississippi valley behind for scrub oak country that faded off into tall grass prairie and then short grass prairie, is that the shorter the grass gets, the bluer the sky becomes, and the more deceiving distances can be. I walked beside my oxen leading my wagon towards that line of cottonwoods for the entire morning and most of the afternoon without getting there. We made slow progress as we climbed up and down the shallow hills I had come to recognize as sand dunes frozen in place by grass roots and sage brush and other prairie plants. I wondered at how this land must have been different in the past, maybe due to lack of rainfall lasting long enough for the grass to die and for the sand to blow up into barren hills that would march slowly eastward with the prevailing winds until the rains came again and the grass returned and locked the dunes in place again. My reading of Charles Lyell's writings had taught me to think about such things and to see the land never stays the same even though in our limited view of things it seems unchangeable.

By late afternoon, the western sky had turned dark with thunderclouds more foreboding than the previous few nights' displays. Massive white clouds rose in giant billowing columns to the northwest, reflecting the low sunlight that was completely blocked by the clouds to the west and southwest. A brisk, cool wind whipped up as I finally descended into a shallow creek bed lined with cottonwoods, whose leaves rustled energetically in the wind. The wind picked up and the smaller branches waved back and forth as they shed some of their leaves, a few of which had already turned bright yellow, reminding me autumn was not far off and winter was coming right behind it.

Far-off lightning sent low thunder rolling towards me across the waving grass. Soon the lightning was coming closer and the thunder was cracking all around me. Thick curtains of rain fell from the low clouds. Big cold raindrops spattered the wagon canvas and rolled off the brim of my hat.

I like to imagine I saw a great flash of bright light with a simultaneous hammer of thunder just after the dollar-sized hail started pelting the trees and my oxen and my outfit, but the fact is I don't remember anything following the thump of the first hailstones except a void. I can't even say it was a black void, or that I felt my heart pounding or blood rushing through my ears, or that I dreamed of flying high in the sky and looking down at my body lying on the ground next to my dead oxen. There was simply . . . nothing.

I awakened slowly, like swimming up through a scummy pond and seeing the sunlight grow brighter as the air bubbles streamed out my mouth and nose and past my face and neck as I struggled not to breathe before breaking into daylight. I found myself lying beneath a buffalo robe with my head propped up on a pile of folded blankets. My head throbbed. Light from a flickering campfire lit up my wagon canvas and the face of a man wearing a beaver hat, a shirt closed at the collar with a bolo tie, and a long black overcoat. He had high cheekbones and dark eyes. His face was a light leathery brown, framed by shoulder-length black hair. There was a trace of a mustache on his upper lip.

He stood up and leaned over me so his face disappeared into shadow, but I still saw his mouth break into a wry grin.

"I'm the goddam Indian," he said. "Good to see you back with the living."

He sat back into a squat and stirred the embers with a stick.

I lay there quiet, trying to clear my head and make sense of the scene before me.

"Don't bother with formal introductions," he said. "Just call me Pete and I will call you Jed."

I tried to sit up straight, but my dizziness and the weight of the buffalo robe seemed like obstacles too large for effective action. I eased back and let my eyelids close for a moment before I opened them again.

"What happened to me? How do you know my name?" I asked.

"Lightning," he answered.

"And," he continued, "I heard Clint and that beautiful black-haired girl call you Jed two or three times each while you were burying your dead back up the trail a bit. So, I surmised Jed must be your name. Then, I saw your given name written in your family Bible—Jedediah P. Carpenter."

"What?? You've been poking around in my things?"

"Sorry, I just got bored. I especially enjoyed thumbing through your volumes by Emerson and Thoreau. And, your family Bible is quite impressive, although I'm not sure carrying its weight half-way across the continent is justified by the messages within. There are some funny and interesting stories in it, though. You've taken your sweet time waking up."

"How long?"

"Three days."

"The oxen?"

"Dead."

"Damn," I said. I didn't usually use swear words, at least not way back then, but this situation seemed to call for a few.

"I hope you don't mind," Pete expanded, "but I traded them on your behalf to my people. Seemed a shame to let perfectly good meat and leather go to waste."

"Oh. Sure," I said. "What did I get for them?"

"That robe you're lying under," he answered, "ten pounds of fresh beef waiting to dry into jerky, some green ox leather and sinew, and my company for a few days."

"Great," I said, and thought to myself I wasn't sure whether my situation had improved any since the lightning struck, or not.

"So, who are your people?" I asked. I was finally well enough to sit up straight and lean back against my hands in the sand.

"Arapaho," he said. "On my mother's side. My father's from Mexico. He is in the fur trade out of Santa Fe."

"So he's a trapper?" I asked. I had read a lot about beaver trappers and the fur trade throughout the Rockies from New Mexico all the way up into Canada and had always wanted to talk to some real trappers. I knew beaver were already getting scarce in some parts of the Rockies, just like they had been trapped almost to nonexistence in the east over the past century.

"No, he just trades. Doesn't like to get his hands dirty and prefers sleeping in a warm bed, I suppose," Pete explained.

"You don't look much like an Indian," I observed. Back then, I was young and fairly stupid and tended to say whatever came to mind, when I chose to speak at all, without considering the ramifications of my words. Fortunately, Pete didn't take offense at my direct approach. He glanced up at me and then stirred the fire for a minute or two before he responded.

"No, but I can dress up like one and fit right in any time I want to," he said. "I've been in St. Louis for the past few years, attending the white man schools and handling business for my father on that end. I'm heading to Cherry Creek to stay with my mother's people a while; maybe drift southeast with them to the Washita country for the winter. My parents wanted me to be able to move about in both worlds—all three, actually—white English-speaking America, brown Spanish-speaking Santa Fe, and my mother's culture, too."

"Sounds like an interesting life," I said.

"It has been," he said.

"How did you hear Clint talking to me the other day?"

"Wasn't only the other day," he said and laughed quietly. "I like to make a game out of crawling into people's camps without getting caught. That day, I was lying in the grass in front of the rocky outcropping about twenty feet from your sister's grave. There were four or five other times I hung around your campsites between Fort Kearny and here. Once I even took a nap in the black-haired girl's—Emma, you called her—wagon when she and her parents went off to bathe in the Platte."

"Seems mighty risky," I said.

"Only if I ever get caught, which I never intend to do," he chuckled. "Fact is, I like making fools of white men. Mexicans and Indians, too, for that matter. My mother's people call me Scares-the-Ponies. That's not my real Arapaho name, but I like it when they call me by it."

I looked at him without saying anything, then he continued, "I was on a raiding party up in Crow territory when I was about your age—must have been about five years ago—and I determined to sneak into a Crow camp to steal their horses in the night before they could wake up and catch me. What happened was, I saw one of them on watch, sleeping like the dead in the midst of their horses. He had a Colt revolver in his belt. Well, I decided I wanted that revolver as bad as I wanted to steal their horses, so I crept up and eased it out of his belt. Problem was, as I lifted it towards me, I got my thumb tangled up with the trigger and the damn thing went off. It didn't hit anything important, but it made a hell of racket. We were down in a narrow canyon and the sound of that shot seemed to echo off the rocks for half the night. All seven of the horses in that camp scattered like they'd been snake-bit. I couldn't catch a single one. But, the Crow never saw me in their camp despite all the ruckus. And, I still have that Colt revolver."

I've known quite a few Arapaho and Cheyenne and Utes over the years, and Pete Scares-the-Ponies is the only one I have ever met who told me most of his life story in the first hour I knew him. Most of them don't say much, if anything, when I am around, at least not until they've known me for a few years. Maybe Pete talked so much because he had already been around me for a couple of months, whether I knew it or not, and because I didn't try to talk his head off with my own stories, of which I had very few back then.

"So what's your real Arapaho name?" I asked when we had both been quiet for a while.

"Only six people in the world know my real name," he said, "and none of us speak it out loud. Speaking of names, to my people you are Calls-the-Thunder," then he repeated the name in his native Arapaho tongue which sounded so strange to me then I could not even make out any distinct syllables in his speech. "It is a name with grave import and power," he continued, "and will command respect among all of the people of the plains. It won't be long before the tribes from the Comanche to the south to the Lakota and Blackfeet in the north have all heard your story. When you identify yourself by that name, they will know you once helped my people by providing food, even if ox meat is far inferior to buffalo, with the help of the Great Spirit. "

I looked at him skeptically, not knowing whether he was playing a joke on me, but I kind of liked the idea of being known far and wide as a provider of food and a friend of the Great Spirit. His words may have helped determine the course of my life. I did not have many occasions to introduce myself as Calls-the-Thunder, but his words turned out to be true: every Indian who heard this name seemed to know the story behind it without my having to explain a thing.

"I like it," I said. "And thank you for taking care of me these past few days. By the way, in all of your rooting around in my wagon, did you happen to come across any beans or flour or cornmeal?"

Scares-the-Ponies chuckled and said, "If you are hungry, you must be getting better. Sit still and I will bring you some food."

We spent the rest of the evening eating fresh jerky softened in a pot of beans, finished off with cornbread swirled in the pot-liquor, then sitting quietly as the fired died away, watching the dark moonless night come to life with what must have been a billion stars in the bright band of the Milky Way. I saw more stars that night in the dry high plains sky than I ever saw looking up at the misty sky through the hickory and oak trees surrounding my family's cabin on the Mississippi delta in eastern Arkansas.

Pete Scares-the-Ponies, true to his name, did not have a horse there at my camp. He had given the pony he rode from St. Louis to his mother's people to help drag their lodges up the South Platte to Cherry Creek, saying he would follow on foot as soon as I was well. He moved about my camp the next morning in preparation for leaving.

"Jedediah Calls-the-Thunder," he addressed me when he saw I was awake and moving around in reasonable comfort, "you seem well today and it is time I followed my people to the mountain front. If you are going to Oregon, I wish you luck finding a team of oxen or a couple of mules to get you there. I will let anyone I see along my route know they might strike a deal with you if they have some spare livestock."

"Thanks, Pete Scares-the-Ponies," I said. "I will figure something out. I don't plan to spend the winter out here."

He raised his hand in a farewell gesture and headed out. He had a few blankets and some clothing in a bedroll slung over one shoulder. With a knife at his belt, and a bow and a quiver of arrows slung over his other shoulder, he could travel lightly on foot and provide for himself along the way.

So, there I was, in the late summer of 1858, with a fully outfitted wagon, tools, and farm supplies, but no oxen to pull it anywhere. I began to reconsider my plans for continuing west on the Oregon Trail. I was fifteen hundred miles from Oregon with winter peering over the horizon, but only a couple of hundred miles from the confluence of Cherry Creek and the South Platte. I knew enough about the California gold rush of 1849 to know I had a rare opportunity to be at the start of something big, if I chose to go southwest rather than west from my stranded campsite in Nebraska Territory. As soon as spring arrived, I knew there would be a flood of white men from the east pouring into western Kansas Territory hoping to strike it rich. If I got there the autumn before the human onslaught arrived, I could be well positioned to take advantage of the situation.

I decided to follow Pete. I figured I could give the new gold camps a try for a year or so and if things didn't work out, I could always head for Oregon the following spring. But first, I had to figure out what to do with my cargo. I certainly couldn't pull the wagon myself, but I was determined not to leave my family's belongings stranded on the prairie for the likes of Zeke Jones to carry off.

My outfit was parked right where it was when the lightning struck, in the edge of a clump of tall cottonwood trees stretching out as far as I could see along a dry meandering creek bed. I spent half of that day exploring until I found a dry gully that angled off into some sand hills to the northeast. I wanted to get my things as far from the Trail as I could, but I didn't want to leave them exposed to spring floods or in an obvious place any wandering hunter could stumble upon. I followed the gully up into the sand hills until its banks cut vertically into layers of limestone. The gully ended in a shallow box canyon sheltering a thicket of cottonwoods, willows, chokecherries and a dozen other varieties of small trees and shrubs I did not have names for.

I spent the rest of the afternoon shuttling tools, clothing, pots, pans, and sacks of seeds from my family's wagon to that box canyon. I piled them all together in a small clearing I found in the thicket. I cut a big piece of the canvas from the wagon and used it to cover my pile of worldly goods. I hoped it would all be safe over the winter. I also hoped I could find it again if I ever made it back there to retrieve any of it. Walking back to my camp, I bemoaned the fact that the job would have been a hell of a lot easier with a wheel-barrow or small cart to transport the things in.

That gave me the idea to tear down my wagon and build a handcart from the parts. I went back to my cache in the box canyon and retrieved a saw, hammer, drill and a few other tools. By the time the sun went down, I was hard at work measuring and sawing and hammering. I built a bright fire from cottonwood branches and wagon scraps so I could work in the dark. By first light I had my creation finished: a handcart made with one wagon wheel in the front and long handles extending out back just like a large wheelbarrow. A big cargo box secured above the handles had two folding legs I could kick with my feet to store them out of the way for traveling, or to lock in a downward position for resting the vehicle on three points—two legs and the front wheel.

I tested my handcart empty, pushing it up the shallow dunes lining the creek bed. and then maneuvering it back to the box canyon loaded with some of the left over wagon parts and hardware. I found it was easier in most cases, especially in deep sand, to pull it rather than to push it, but in either case it was well balanced and quite handy.

I then gave careful thought to what I would need on Cherry Creek and began to pack it all onto the cargo box. Carpenter tools were a necessity, as I figured to earn my way in part by building for the incoming prospectors when I wasn't out staking claims for myself. Extra clothing, including my warm sheepskin coat, my newly-acquired buffalo robe, a bag of mixed vegetable seeds, ten pounds of cornmeal and ten pounds of beans, some of the leather wagon harness rigging, some beef jerky and my father's rifle and ammunition rounded out my load. I secured my cargo with the remains of my wagon canvas and rope to keep it secure from wind and rain. I left most of my cache behind, a hundred pounds of beans and flour, the water barrel, spare wagon parts, all of the clothing that belonged to my parents and sister, and all of the household furniture we had not left behind on the trail—I hadn't told Zeke Jones how many things we had thrown overboard since we left the Mississippi river behind.

When I grabbed the handles intending to set out for Cherry Creek, I could barely lift the load and in no way could see pushing or pulling it more than a few feet. So, I considered my design for a few minutes, unloaded everything, and removed the cargo box. I mounted it much closer to the wheel, with a flat extension out over the wheel for longer items, then loaded all of my things back onto it, with the heaviest items pushed as far forward as I could place them. I put the canvas back on and secured it with the rope.

This time I easily lifted the handles, kicked the legs into the up position, and headed back down the gully out of the box canyon. I was pretty proud of myself—my ingenuity and skill with tools would have made my father happy, I thought. I didn't think about it too long, though, because thinking of my family made me sad and made me realize I was completely alone in the world. I also couldn't think very hard about much of anything, because no matter how well-constructed my handcart was and no matter how well I balanced and stowed the cargo, it was going to be damn hard work pushing and pulling that outfit up the hills and over the creek beds and across the plains between there and Cherry Creek. I knew from the rough maps I had seen that I had to climb a full two thousand feet in elevation to get where I was going, and that fact just did not bear thinking about.

I followed the Platte west, headed for the place where the South Platte and North Platte forked, with the South branch trending southwest towards Cherry Creek. I reckoned I was just a few days from the confluence of the two Plattes, but deep sand and weary muscles slowed my progress. By the time I got there, it was early September. I had another idea for my handcart along the way. I made camp near the river among some cottonwoods on the south bank of the South Platte and settled in to rest and work. I slept more than might be reasonable, caught some fish in the river, and dawdled for three days until I was completely rested and ready to head for the mountains. During those days I took the leather oxen harness parts apart and restitched them into a harness for myself. When I was strapped into my new rigging, my hips took most of the weight of my outfit off my arms, so the going became much easier.

On the fourth morning in my camp at the mouth of the South Platte, I awoke before dawn with an uneasy feeling I was being watched. I sat up straight and looked around. Pete Scares-the-Ponies sat on a cottonwood log not ten feet from me, his devilish grin outlining white teeth reflecting the full moon's bright light from low in the western sky.

"Well, damn my hide," I said—my language was growing in shades of color as I made progress towards what I thought was instant fortune in the gold fields—and chuckled. "It's the goddam Indian."

Pete nodded my direction and said, "I've been leaving sign around your camp for three days any fool could read if he just paid attention. It's tough country out here, boy. You'd better wake up and watch your backside. And your front side, for that matter."

We stirred up the fire and cooked cornbread in the growing morning light. After breakfast and a hot mug of tea, I set about packing up my gear and getting ready to hit the trail again. Pete walked over to the horse he now had, hobbled among the trees. I had not heard a sound in the night to indicate I had company, human or equine or otherwise. I like to blame the laughter of the river flowing nearby for my lack of awareness, but the bald fact is I was just young and stupid. And exceedingly lucky.

Pete returned and held out his hands to me. He held a bow and a half dozen arrows.

"These are yours," he said. "A gift from my people. The bow is from a bois d'arc tree, from a Cherokee craftsman down in Indian Territory. The arrows are from my mother's brother, who has a fine pair of moccasins made from your ox hide."

I took the bow and arrows from Pete, overwhelmed by his generosity. "Thank you, Pete," I said. "But, what am I supposed to do with these? Knock chokecherries down from high branches? Poke a rabbit in the butt and make him hop faster?"

"Maybe when you get tired of cornbread, you will figure it out. Or, we could travel together to Cherry Creek and I could teach you how to hunt, and how to make your own arrows," he offered.

"I would like that. By the way, where'd you get the horse?" I asked.

"My mother's brother loaned her to me. He got her from a Ute scout up on the Cache la Poudre who didn't need her anymore." He grinned at me and set to work packing up his bedroll.

I contemplated the implications of his answer without asking for expansion or clarification.

We spent the next two weeks slowly moving southwest. Pete taught me how to hunt along the way. First I practiced with un-tipped arrow shafts just to get the feel of the bow, using cactus clumps or cottonwood trunks as targets. We cut thin branches from willows in the thickets near the river and he taught me how to straighten them into perfectly balanced shafts. He showed me how to make a bowstring with ox sinew and how to lash the iron arrow points to the willow shafts with the same material.

"It's not as good as buffalo," he said, "but we will use what we have to use." Pete Scares-the-Ponies told me he had visions that told him his mother's way of life was on its way into the history books along with the millions of buffalo they depended on for food, clothing and shelter. I don't know if his insights came directly from the Great Spirit or if he was just a really smart man, but in not many years I saw his visions becoming real. In not many years after that, the buffalo had been hunted almost to extinction by white men with rifles.

"I thought arrowheads were knapped from flint," I observed as he tied a point securely to a shaft.

He chuckled and said, "I guess some Crow elders still make their own arrowheads using stone-age techniques, but I buy mine by the pound down at Bent's Fort on the Arkansas River. I can get a year's supply in exchange for one beaver pelt."

Early one morning, when the sun was still an unformed thought in the brightening eastern sky, I made my first kill— a mallard duck swimming in a quiet pool beyond a willow thicket where I hid on the riverbank. When my arrow flew into his breast just below his neck, the sound spooked the rest of the birds. The shallows erupted into the thunder of hundreds of wing beats as ducks, geese and herons all lit out for safer water upstream.

Pete and I had juicy fire-roasted duck for breakfast that morning before we headed back out on the trail. Over the next few days, I sharpened my hunting skills. Ducks, geese, catfish, and rabbits all fell beneath my aim, and Pete stood approvingly aside while I fed the two of us in a manner that soon became routine for me. Before long, I added a pronghorn antelope to our list of meals, a feat which included several hours of tracking and stalking to get close enough to the swift beast for a shot before he was alerted to my scent. Without Pete Scares-the-Ponies teaching me, I would never have attempted such a kill. In fact, without his help, I probably would have died somewhere in western Nebraska Territory and added my bones to the collection of white man's trash littering the trail.

As we ate pronghorn stew one evening, Pete paid me his greatest compliment. "You learn fast. You have become a passable hunter."

"I've had a good teacher," I responded. The fact is I have never enjoyed killing. I liked it even less way back then. It is one of my life's ironies that my skill with a bow and arrow, and with my father's rifle, ended up getting me far more gold than prospecting ever did. I had no way of knowing that at the time, when I put on a stern exterior look so Pete would not see me washed in guilt and sadness every time I took the life of a creature whose bad fortune led her into my path.

We had to eat, and the beans and flour and cornmeal lasted much longer when we had meat to go with them, but I learned over the years to supplement my meals with wild plants and fruits whenever I could, so I would not have to kill so many animals for myself. Hunting for cash was another matter, and I did what needed doing.

The worst time was a year or two later, up in South Park, when I shot a mule deer doe from near the limit of my bow and arrow range. I came up to her and saw it was not a clean kill. She lay in the grass staring at me with her infinitely deep dark eyes, her nostrils wet with blood as her chest heaved in slow gasps for air. I finished her with my knife and then noticed a pair of spotted fawns looking at me from across the tall grass at the edge of the meadow, their over-long ears cocked forward, with fearful curiosity in their eyes.

The perspective a person gets by approaching the Rockies on foot is far different than that of those who arrive in Denver for the first time by train. Walking for two weeks after the first peaks appear on the horizon gives an understanding of the vastness of things that a few hours by train distorts into a sense of smallness first-time visitors are cheated by. There were no trains in this part of the world in 1858, so I got the better experience, by approaching the Front Range on foot.

My first sight of the mountains came at dawn one crisp September morning when the rising sun lit up the highest peaks like tented lanterns on the horizon. The previous afternoon and evening had been cloudy in the west, so I had not noticed the change in the view as we made our way southwest keeping the valley of the South Platte off to our right. It was easier following faint game trails and sometimes well-trodden paths worn by trappers and Indians, up on the rolling plains east of the river than it was to follow right alongside the river's banks. Getting a steady supply of water would have been nice, but the higher route avoided numerous creek beds and steep-walled gullies feeding into the river.

So, we were camped on a broadly sloping hillside high above the river that morning when I first saw the Rockies. The dawn-filtered sunlight, clear air, and the massive height of the mountains made them look near enough for me to reach in an hour or two if I took off in a bee-line trot their direction. The reality, though, was we were still almost a hundred miles and two weeks of slow progress with my handcart through deep sand and over rocky creek beds away from the foothills that marked the western edge of the plains. By late September, we had a breathtaking panorama taking in Pikes Peak far away to the south and Long's Peak due west, with the mountain that would become known as Mount Evans in between, the backdrop to our destination at the mouth of Cherry Creek.

It took Pete Scares-the-Ponies and me until early October to reach our destination at the mouth of Cherry Creek where it flows into the South Platte. Pete could have made the journey from the mouth of the South Platte up to its confluence with Cherry Creek in just a few days on his horse, but my pace with the handcart and my time spent hunting determined our slow pace. I never asked Pete to let me hitch my cart to his horse, even though the idea occurred to me early on in our time on the trail together. I think he took a fiendish delight in watching a skinny kid work so hard to transport things he himself would have had little use for. In any case, by the time we reached our final stopping place, I was as strong and sinewy as the oxen whose place I had taken a month before.

Much to my disappointment, though, I had not grown in height since my family set out from St. Louis. I always envisioned myself growing to a height sufficient to dominate any other man I met, which might explain my bravado in telling Zeke Jones what I would do to him if he mistreated Emma Cooper. But, I arrived on Cherry Creek fully grown, as it turned out, carrying my full adult height of five feet three inches. It was all right, though. I learned to make my way in the world quite well by using my wiry scrawniness and quick wit together to satisfactory effect.

That late fall of 1858 was a wonderful time to be camped out at the base of the Front Range along the banks of the various creeks and rivers flowing into the South Platte. When Pete and I arrived, there were not only the remnants of William Green Russell's prospecting party, consisting of several grizzled white men and their Cherokee compatriots from Georgia, but there were also thirty Arapaho lodges and at least fifty lodges of the Cheyenne, tall tipis of finely tanned skins (although, even then, a few of them were canvas-covered in lieu of leather) secured around conical frames of lodge poles, with smoke-hole openings in the tops.

As early as the day we arrived, a steady trickle of prospectors was coming in from every direction: trappers from the high mountains, merchants or laborers from Taos and Santa Fe, and even a few immigrants who caught wind of the gold strike and diverted their wagons from the Oregon Trail or Mormon Trail and headed south to strike it rich instead of continuing on to Salt Lake or Oregon to earn an honest living tilling the soil and building lasting communities.

I asked around about Clint Williams and found a few men who knew him, but of course he had not had time to get all the way to St. Louis and back. I hoped I would see him the following spring after the snow melted.

The prospectors had built a few rude cabins along the course of Cherry Creek and up the South Platte a ways, mostly with canvas sheets for walls and roofs, but three or four with substantial log walls and hand-hewn shake roofs. They had already organized a town called Auraria on the west creek bank, and it wasn't long before a rival town, soon called Denver City, sprang up on the opposite bank.

Pete encouraged me to stay with his people for the winter, but I knew they were going to leave soon to winter in the far south along the Arkansas River or even farther east and I didn't want to leave the gold camp. So, I stayed with him for a week or so and then moved my things to a level meadow sheltered by cottonwood trees by the edge of a creek I followed several miles towards the mountains from the main prospector camp. From reading the work of Charles Lyell, I deduced the really rich placers and lode veins, if such could be found, were more likely to be in the mountains than out there on the edge of the plains, so I planned to do some quiet prospecting on my own before winter set in, up in the mountains and out of sight of the others. By setting up my camp away from everybody else, I took on some of the risks that come with solitary living, but I gained the advantage of privacy in my goings and comings.

Pete came to visit me before his people moved south. We sat around my campfire into the late evening and early night darkness, poking at embers with sticks and watching sparks rise into the heavens.

"Pete Scares-the-Ponies," I said at one point when the quiet grew heavy around us, "I think we work well together. Maybe you could stay here and we could go prospecting up in the mountains before the snow flies, or next spring after the melt."

He considered my words in silence while he added more wood to the fire and stirred it to bring back the flames.

"I could do that," he said. "But, the mountains are generally considered to be Ute territory. As an Arapaho, I might find myself getting distracted from prospecting in order to kill Utes. I prefer living peacefully, so it is best for me to move along with my mother's people."

I could see the wisdom in what he said, but I wasn't ready to give up on having him for a prospecting partner.

"Don't go as Arapaho, then," I suggested. "When you dress in your American clothes, you can easily pass for a white man. Then you would not have to fight the Utes just because your mother is Arapaho."

He grunted and looked up at me from his crouched position by the fire. "No, if I went as a white man, I might find myself killing Utes for no good reason at all."

So, we parted ways. I saw Pete from time to time over the next few years, sometimes in the saloons or on the streets of Auraria and Denver and Golden, and once or twice when I was out on the prairie hunting.

The last time I saw Pete—I didn't recognize it was him at first—he was lying over a little Cheyenne girl in a dry wash that led up from Big Sandy Creek, way out on the prairie almost two hundred miles southeast of Denver. It was late November, but the air was as cold as you'd expect in mid-January, and filled with the stench of black powder smoke. I suppose there was occasional cannon fire and the confusion of excited horsemen all around, but I don't remember hearing any of that as I stared down into the creek bed.

The girl's face had dust-streaked tear tracks leading from her eyes down her checks and onto her neck, but she was not making any sound—she must have been about five years old —peering out at me from beneath Pete's chest. I saw a small round hole in the back of his coat that was oozing a thin trail of blood.

I scrambled down the sandy bank and through hip-deep snow drifted into the shadows to pull his lifeless body off of the girl. In turning him over, I realized who it was. I cried out in anguish, kneeled and pounded my fists into the sand, then took long, slow breaths until I could function normally again. I scooped the little girl into my arms—the silent terror in her eyes is seared into my memory to this day like a cattle brand —and hurried up the wash, alternately padding through deep loose sand, then crunching through the thin crust atop deep snow drifts, until I found signs in the sand leading to some of her people hiding in the dense brush beside a dry sandbar inside a broad curve in the bank.

In my finest broken Cheyenne, which was not very good, I called softly to them, "I am Calls-the-Thunder. I bring you this girl, a gift from Scares-the-Ponies, who gave his life to save hers. I am so sorry for this day and for the way my people have treated you." A woman rose from the bushes and took two strides to me and gently took the girl from my arms. She turned and disappeared back into the snow-laden brush without a sound.

I'm getting ahead of my story by relating this now, but my time is short and I wanted it written that I was there that morning on the 29th of November in 1864—how and why I came to be there with the First Colorado Regiment is a long story worthy of many pages of its own in my narrative—but neither I nor any of the members of Captain Silas Soule's Company D fired a shot into the quiet Cheyenne and Arapaho camp that lay below us as the sun rose on that cold, snow-cursed morning. I spoke earlier of memories like a frozen river that never change despite the enshrouding fog of passing decades. My memories of this day are like that, too, so vivid I sometimes wish I could melt them with a torch and let them flow away from me, to be diluted into insignificance in an ocean beyond some faraway delta.

I sometimes try to remember the last time I saw Pete alive and what we said to each other, but no clear picture emerges. We probably shared a drink or two, or maybe we were both out on the prairie hunting, but wherever we were I am sure neither of us spoke any words that penetrated beneath the surface of things. That is one of the regrets I will soon leave behind.

Before the heavy snows came in the fall of 1858, I accomplished many things. I honed my skills as a hunter and provided meat for the growing gold camps, first in exchange for a gold pan and some other prospecting tools, later in exchange for cash or gold dust. One of the most valuable things I traded for in those early days was a mule I called Fred. He was a little lame in one leg when I got him from Edmund Tanner in exchange for a brace of wild turkeys in hand plus a promise of regularly-provided meat for the month of November. I treated Fred well and let him rest at my camp for several weeks until his leg healed. After that, he was a loyal companion and beast of burden for many years. Fred and I, working together, could carry many times more slaughtered game back into the gold camps than I could manage on my own, and he tirelessly provided muscle-power and transport for my prospecting and carpentering enterprises over the years.

I fanned out from my camp, first alone and then with Fred, and learned the lay of the land in a broad circle, out on the prairie to the east and up into the foothills to the west. I didn't venture into the high mountains that first fall, because they were already cloaked with snow by the time Pete and I arrived at Cherry Creek. But I did get to know several of the major drainages feeding the Platte and I kept mental notes on all of the best hunting areas, a few good places to plant vegetable seeds in the spring, and a half dozen likely creeks for prospecting.

In late November, the bitingly cold night air and increasingly frequent snowfalls told me it was time to build a camp more permanent than the canvas-covered lean-to I had been staying in. I found an open meadow, undoubtedly formed by sediment filling in beaver ponds over the centuries, not far up the canyon formed by what the prospectors were calling Bear Creek. It was a perfect spot for a big garden in the spring, with plentiful water nearby, adequate pasture for Fred and a southerly exposure that would allow adequate daylight. I found plentiful chokecherries, wild plums and raspberry thickets along the creek banks mixed with a variety of willows, cottonwoods, ash and other plants that would provide cover for wildlife and cover for me when I was stalking them. The northern, south-facing slopes leading down to the creek were dry with arid plants like prickly pears and yuccas in clumps breaking up the autumn-brown grass, but the southern, north-facing slopes, which rarely got intense sunshine, hosted a rich forest of fir and spruce trees.

With Fred's generous assistance and my father's tools, I cut down trees and hewed them into square logs, then hauled them back to my clearing for building a small one-room cabin with a cozy sleeping loft above the ceiling joists. I left the floor bare dirt, thinking that someday I might put in pine plank flooring, but I didn't end up staying there long enough to worry about such amenities. I framed the roof with sturdy timbers and covered it with thin spruce shingles. I didn't take time to build a fireplace and chimney, but instead laid out a stone hearth in the center of the room. I left a smoke-hole at the peak of the roof, taking the idea for my design from the Arapaho and Cheyenne lodges I had seen down on Cherry Creek.

I built a lean-to shed on each end of the cabin, one for stacked firewood and the other, with walls enclosed in canvas, as a shelter for Fred. We settled in for the winter. As November gave way to December I realized I hadn't even noticed my seventeenth birthday when it passed in the midst of my ramblings in early September.

One of my fondest and most exciting memories from the spring of 1859 is my first view of South Park from Kenosha Hill. In late May, I followed the North Fork of the South Platte upstream, past the places now called Bailey and Shawnee and up the canyon to the top of the pass. As I mounted Kenosha Hill from the east, I followed the river to its source, where it is lost in a series of beaver ponds nestled among groves of aspen and spruce trees. The ground was littered with winter-trodden aspen leaves among deep drifts of fresh snow as I followed the gentle rise of the hill through thick stands of spruce and fir. I was in the depths of a seemingly unending forest when I began a shallow descent down the western side of the pass, following a well-worn foot path that must have seen the passing of wildlife and men for thousands of years before me. Suddenly, I emerged from the trees and saw the most startling and beautiful panorama I had ever seen in my short life up until then. Imagine a seventeen-year-old Arkansas orphan boy standing at an elevation close to ten thousand feet, with a snowy spring forest behind him and an expanse of grassland ringed by snow-capped mountains before him stretching as far as he could see.

I stood with wonder at the spectacle, my mouth agape, Fred snuffling beside me. There are many places in Colorado with more magnificent vistas, but this was new land to me. My Mississippi Delta background had offered nothing to prepare me for it. In the gentle rolling grassland I could envision bison and deer and elk and bears and small game to sustain a livelihood, and I saw in the encircling high mountains a lifetime of places for prospecting, maybe even places to strike it rich.

I stopped there that day in the edge of the forest overlooking South Park, contemplated the view for a good half hour, then turned back, knowing I would return as soon as I could. That view from Kenosha Hill sealed my fate. I was mesmerized by the territory spread out before me that would become the heart of the new state of Colorado in not many years. Gazing at that scene, I knew I had found my own personal paradise, which I would spend every moment possible exploring and learning to live in and to love for the rest of my life. I knew I would spend the rest of my life doing whatever was necessary to ensure I was never more than a few days' ride from that magical lookout point.

As I made my way back down the pass on the route towards Bear Creek, I met five or six prospecting parties headed towards South Park. Acting on stories told by trappers around winter campfires about color in the creeks throughout the Park, and disappointed in the limited extent of the Cherry Creek strike, they were heading out early hoping to stake claims before the snow-melt was over. I wished them well and told them I would be heading back that way before long, ready to strike it rich, or to take their gold in exchange for fresh meat, or to take their gold in games of chance, or all three, depending upon the circumstances.

I reached the edge of my clearing on Bear Creek about sundown on a day in late May after being gone for about two weeks. I was tired and Fred was ready to shed his load to loaf in the rich spring grass, so I didn't see or smell the smoke curling up from my cabin's smoke-hole or the clearly visible human and horse tracks in the mud below melting snow-drifts. I unloaded my gear and turned Fred loose to graze in the meadow, then opened the cabin door, expecting cold darkness.

Instead, there was a glowing fire in the hearth and the aroma of roasting meat.

"I see that goddam Indian didn't catch you unawares like I just did," a voice stated from above me in the loft. Clint Williams eased down the ladder and turned to me. His wide grin hid the seriousness of his next words, "You gotta learn to watch your backside, boy, or you're gonna find yourself feeding the turkey buzzards one day soon!"

"You're right about that, Clint," I said as I gave his meaty hand a vigorous shake. "I'm learning, but you caught me tired, I guess. I've been real lucky so far."

"Well, I hope you don't mind me making myself at home. Nice spot you found here, and good work on the cabin. Sit down and share some dinner with me."

So we ate and talked as the dark descended outside the four small unglazed windows facing up and down the canyon, and overlooking the creek in the back and the meadow in the front. I pulled the canvas covers down over the window openings. My eyes adjusted to the flickering light from the fire. I enjoyed the close warmth of the cabin after two weeks of spending cold spring nights sleeping on spruce boughs covering the frozen ground and slogging through deep snow in the high country.

I described my view from Kenosha Hill and told Clint about my plans for spending the summer hunting and prospecting. His tired eyes gazed at me from across the fire and I think I noticed that evening for the first time how old Clint was. His hair was silver-gray, parted in the middle and swept back behind his ears as it fell to his shoulders. His bushy brows were still black, but deep wrinkles lined the corners of his eyes. Dark spots mottled the backs of his hands. When he got up to stir the beans in the pot, he moved with the caution of an elderly man, unlike the energetic frontier scout I had come to know on the Oregon Trail the year before.

"Your plans sound mighty exciting, Jed," he said when I paused to pull a bite from the roasted wild turkey wing on my plate, "and I would like to go out with you every chance I get. But, the fact is I'm not young any more. I lit out for St. Louis last summer like a young colt, expecting to put together a grubstake and be out here by April striking it rich. But the winter wore me down and the trip out here told me it might be time to slow down a mite. So, I have a proposition for you."

"Go on," I said, peering across a spoonful of beans at him.

"I'm thinking of settling down in one spot for a while. Resting up, taking it easy. Now it occurs to me you might need some of the prospecting gear I brought from St. Louis, and it also occurs to me you have built yourself a mighty cozy place here with good water and fine garden soil, and it also occurs to me, if you are going to be gone all summer tramping about you will have little use for this place or the seeds your Mama packed out here all the way from Arkansas. So, I'm thinking about a trade."

"Go on," I said again, being tired and not at the height of my limited conversational skill.

"How about this," he said. "Let me stay here and plant some potatoes and squash and beans and tomatoes. I will spend my time reading some of those deep books you've collected on that shelf yonder while I keep the deer out of the garden and trade with passersby for cash money, ammunition or gold dust in exchange for fresh vegetables and the occasional trout. You're bound to be situated here on a prime route to the gold fields, if any be found up there in the high mountains, so I figure there are ample opportunities for commerce for a cantankerous old man sitting in a rocking chair on the front porch of a tidy cabin in such a fine setting. Don't worry about the rocking chair and porch—I'm fairly handy with tools myself and can already see them in my mind even though they ain't built yet."

I asked Clint, "I can see how you could benefit from my homesteading work and my mother's foresight in bringing seeds west, but what's in it for me?"

"We can be partners," he said. "I'll give you all the prospecting gear and trail food I arrived here with and send you on your way back into the hills with the secure knowledge that your little place here is in good hands. I will split any profits I make on this end—cash money and gold nuggets and so forth—and you will do the same for me from any proceeds you accrue in the gold camps. And, any time you are down this way you will have free lodging and a shed for your mule."

"That's a deal I can live with," I said. So we shook on it. Clint ended up staying there on Bear Creek for another twenty years before he fell through thin ice one winter on a beaver pond just up the canyon. His sister and one of her grandsons were visiting from back east to celebrate Clint's 85th birthday—they came in to Denver the easy way, of course, by train—and he was showing the boy how to catch trout through a hole sawed in the ice. The boy (I call him a boy, but my guess is he was close to forty, still single and occupied with touring his grandmother, who had made quite a fortune speculating in the stock market, around the world to exotic places like the Cape of Good Hope and Denver, Colorado) and his grandmother managed to drag Clint out of the icy water in time to save him from drowning or dying of the cold. He caught pneumonia and died a week later.

Over the years, our partnership lasted without any arguments or suspicions of unfair dealing by either party. Our little place on Bear Creek probably made more money by selling fresh vegetables to passing prospectors and sheep-herders and cattle ranchers than I ever made in the gold fields, but in neither arena of enterprise did we make much money. I suppose if we had made a lot of money, we might have ended up fighting over it. We mostly enjoyed the land— Clint on his little farm and me roaming the mountains before I finally settled here on Buckskin Creek—and prospered in ways that provided our sustenance with little cash required. Those were good times for me. I mourn their passing.

Gold prospecting is a fairly simple process, and in many respects life as a prospector beats the living hell out of a lot of other occupations I can enumerate. The only tools required are a gold pan, a pick, a shovel, and some basic knowledge about minerals, geology and the general lay of the land. Anybody who listens well can pick up valuable tips in a few evenings in a saloon frequented by men, and women— don't want to leave them out, even though lady prospectors were few and far between during the early years of the Pikes Peak gold rush—who claim some success in the enterprise.

The general idea is this: Gold is heavier than most other minerals, so it tends to move downhill from the lode deposits where it rose from deep within the earth millions of years ago, as those deposits are torn apart at their outcroppings on steep mountainsides by snow and ice and wind and rain. Since the gold is dense, it tends to settle out of the streams that carry it downhill whenever the water becomes quiet, where it collects in placer deposits that can be found with a shovel and a gold pan. There is nothing intrinsically gold-bearing about creeks except that creek beds are generally the lowest topographic features around. They are where gravity drops the gold from the lode deposits. Also, creeks have water in them, at least a few months each year, which is a crucial tool in the panning process.

So, in theory, placer deposits will accumulate in low places like creek beds not far downstream of the original lode deposit, along with sand and other detritus on the inside of meanders or at the upstream end of beaver ponds or at places where the water rushes out of tight passageways into a broader valley; anywhere the water's flow slows down.

Prospectors wash sand and gravel from the creek bed or nearby sediment banks and look for "color"—tiny flecks of soft dull yellow gold—in their pans as they work their way upstream into the hills and mountains. A steady increase in "color" as they move upstream, especially an increase in size from dust to nuggets, tells prospectors they are getting close to the original outcropping of gold ore that produced the placer deposit. A sudden disappearance of color from their pans tells the prospectors to climb the last dry gully or side creek or the adjacent mountainsides searching for a quartz vein loaded with gold and other minerals leading deep into the rocks. A "flash in the pan" is what prospectors call it when they get some color that just peters out with no indication of a larger placer deposit or lode deposit nearby.

Many placer deposits were rich gold strikes in their own right, supporting hundreds of claims and not playing out for years, while others amounted to little more than a few days' excitement fueling speculation and claim-jumping and all the orneriness that accompanies any enterprise where dozens of people are all out scratching for themselves.

The gold pan was just a tool the prospectors used to find a gold deposit that might warrant further work. Once a placer strike was confirmed by panning, the main mining would be done with sluice-boxes and long-toms, and in later years as big machines and big capital arrived, with hydraulic mining and dredges that devastated the hillsides and creek bottoms, but were highly effective at paying their investors handsomely for their trouble.

Occasionally, a placer strike would lead to the fabled "mother lode," the Phillips lode above Buckskin Joe being just one example of many that were discovered in the "Pikes Peak country" over the years. I've always thought it a little strange the 1858 gold strike on Cherry Creek led to what all the newspapers called the "Pikes Peak Gold Rush" when the truth is Pikes Peak is a good seventy miles away. I guess Easterners need something to attach their imaginations to, and almost everyone had heard of Pikes Peak way before gold was discovered in the region.

Those were the simple facts about prospecting I learned from William Green Russell's party down on Cherry Creek, along with some knowledge of rock types and depositional characteristics I got from reading Lyell.

What none of my sources dwelled upon is another simple truth: Prospecting is back-breaking, finger-numbing, damn hard work. Because of its density, gold doesn't just sit there on top of the creek bed. looking up at any gold-hungry fool who happens to walk past. It churns deeper into the sediments with every spring flood until it reaches pockets on top of the bedrock. To get to gold-bearing sediments—pay dirt!—a prospector might have to dig down through many feet of barren sand and gravel laid down between massive boulders. The digging itself is hard work and the panning is harder still. Imagine bending over or standing or kneeling in icy cold water, swirling rocks and gravel and sand in a gold pan for hours on end, and finishing the day with little or nothing to show for your efforts. Do this for days or weeks or months without taking a few days off to relax, digging and panning and working your way up a creek bed to its source and finding nothing. Or, striking it rich.

Lode mining was even harder work. A lone miner with a pick and shovel, and later with a hand drill, a sledge hammer and explosives, might make a few feet of progress in a day following an ore vein into the mountainside. If a vein proved to be a paying prospect, miners working around the clock could move several tons of ore a day when they weren't moving timbers and shoring up weak leads or building ladders into dark shafts. It wasn't long before the good claims were bought up by big mining outfits that hired workers for a dollar a day (plus whatever high-grade they could spirit out of the mine undetected)—not bad wages if you didn't take into account the risks of cave-ins, miner's consumption, premature explosions and generally difficult and unpleasant work. I enjoyed the days I devoted to placer mining, but lode mining never appealed to me and I stayed away from it as diligently as I possibly could.

Well, some of us struck it rich in those first months of prospecting in and around South Park. Many of us found nothing but grief out there in the mountains. Some died from the cold. Some died in saloon brawls over whores or card games gone sour. Many went home poorer than when they arrived. Others of us figured out we could make a decent living for ourselves by supplying the needs of the more dedicated, tougher prospectors so they had time for prospecting. I staked a few claims here and there. I always carried my gold pan with me, so I could dawdle anywhere I found myself with some time on my hands to scout out the nearest stream bed.

I always seemed to be a few days late to the really rich strikes, but I found my living by hunting and carpentering and carting corn, beans, potatoes and other fresh vegetables from Clint's farm up into the gold camps and doing anything else that gave me a decent return on my time and effort. I'm even proud to state that most of what I did was generally considered to be legal, with one or two exceptions which might come to light as I continue my narrative.

I helped build the first cabins along Tarryall Creek, and over by Como and up in Fairplay. News of fresh gold discoveries swirled around the camps and seemed to arrive in bunches all summer with every stage coach or freight wagon that rumbled through. While the prospectors were staking their claims and working their fingers into bloody stumps, a real civilization (that's what they call it, but sometimes I'm not so sure) was springing up behind them.

Stores, hotels, saloons, banks, ore smelters, assay offices, newspapers and jailhouses sprung up in the blink of an eye.

It wasn't long after the first rumors of Pikes Peak gold hit the trails east and west that Wells Fargo and the Leavenworth & Pikes Peak Express and others set up regular stagecoach stops on spurs branching off from the Santa Fe, Overland, Smoky Hill and Oregon Trails to head over to Auraria and Denver and points beyond. By the end of the summer of 1859, anybody with ten dollars cash in hand could ride from Denver to Fairplay in two long days inside a fine coach pulled by four horses, but in truth the butt-crunching nature of the ride and the questionable character of the fellow riders and the rather exorbitant fare kept a lot of men like me walking. Most of us had walked a good piece of the way from wherever we came from, so we didn't mind walking once we got here, or riding a horse if we could get one. I will admit after the arrival of the narrow gauge line of the Denver, South Park and Pacific Railroad cut the travel time from Como to Denver down to less than a day in the summer of 1879 I found a new pleasure in not walking from here to there so often.

Miners liked their fun, but it came in ways that might surprise sophisticated easterners who have never bothered to venture west of the Mississippi River. It seems like the first thing to arrive in any mining camp, after the initial rush of picks and shovels and basic necessities like beans and bacon, was an upright piano—how the freight men got a piano all the way from St. Louis or Santa Fe to South Park in one piece is a wonder to me—followed not far behind by the beginnings of a lending library. Certainly the upright pianos came accompanied by taverns stocked with whiskey and dancing girls, and there was general rowdiness and whoring and drunkenness almost any night of the week, but the general level of education among the prospectors and camp followers was surprisingly high. Demand for good books to read and good theater to attend was steady.

I contributed my own collection to the new library in Fairplay and found many hours of satisfaction perusing the other literature offered there. As I said much earlier, I probably contributed a thousand books over the years to the library in Fairplay and others, too. The library in Saints John (so named because the early claimants couldn't agree on which Saint John to name the place after, so they compromised by including them all), up the mountain from Montezuma, comes to mind as a place I rested my sore feet more than once on short, dark winter days when I decided it was too cold outside for any pursuits more worthwhile than expanding my own education. I believe I left my first copy of *Moby Dick* there for others to enjoy.

Besides the libraries and saloons and other public conveniences, there were also theaters and opera houses that sprang up in the places that seemed to have a future beyond the next winter—Denver, Central City, Leadville, and so forth. So, even though the early days in Pikes Peak country were gritty and filled with hardship, it wasn't long before a certain refinement came to the plains and mountains that anybody with the desire to, and sometimes the cash required for entry into, could take advantage of.

In August of that summer Buckskin Joe Higginbottom and I made a big gold discovery on a creek feeding into the Middle Fork of the South Platte a few miles upstream of Fairplay. If I had played my cards right, so to speak, I might have retired a rich man by working my placer claim up there a few miles from Alma, down in the shadows of the Mosquito Range. But, I was young and foolish—this is my excuse for many of my stupidities and misdeeds, even up to the present day, as long as I avoid barroom mirrors and hotel room wash-stand mirrors that remind me I am not still seventeen. I lost my claim in a poker game late one night at Travis McLeod's Snorting Elk Saloon down in Fairplay. I'm not sure the game was entirely honest, but that is the way things went sometimes. I lost my fortune almost as quickly as I found it. I think my life has been happier for it, in any case.

Having never been rich for more than a day or two at a time, I can't speak for those who have built fortunes and lived in circles of society that have never been open to me. But, from my vantage point on the outside, I do believe having a lot of money is not the key to happiness, and might even be an active detriment to it.

Take the example of old H.A.W. (Horace) Tabor, for example. I met him and his fine, albeit somewhat homely, wife Augusta in Oroville, across the pass from Fairplay down near what would become Leadville, late in 1859. They were just setting up shop, as dirt-poor as the rest of us immigrants to the gold fields. H.A.W. and Augusta were shrewd business operators, for sure, but they also impressed me as kind and decent people. She baked bread for sale in their little shop while he ran the rest of the store and pursued backroom deals trading in mining claims. They ran a store in Buckskin Joe for a few years, as well as their various enterprises in the Leadville area.

It wasn't long before Horace and Augusta Tabor were among the richest people in Colorado. Then, along came Baby Doe and their lives came unraveled. H.A.W. fell for the pretty young dance-hall girl and Augusta kicked him out. If he hadn't been rich, maybe Baby Doe wouldn't have found him quite so interesting. If Baby Doe herself hadn't been so in love with money, maybe she wouldn't be living all alone in that little cabin up by the Matchless Mine . . .

But, I'm getting ahead of myself again. The early darkness and the snow piling up outside my cabin, and the racking cough every morning when I get up—I choose not to pay much attention to the blood on the ground after I cough and spit—is making me anxious to get my story down on paper before I decide to walk off into the snow in the light of the full moon one of these fine cold nights. The order of things in my mind gets out of place every now and then and I wander off the track or back up or go ahead before I get all the details filled in.

Joe Higginbottom was one of the more colorful characters in the gold fields that summer and fall. He claimed to be half Shawnee and half free white man, but the rumors following his trail said otherwise. If the stories were true, he was the bastard son of a Mississippi plantation owner by way of a pretty house slave, escaped to the west at a tender age after he rebelled and turned the whip on his master's wife in the midst of a brutal punishment at her hand for some minor infraction. After that event he took up the guise of frontiersman and faded into the prairie with a made-up name and a stolen horse.

Joe was something of a showman who preferred riding his horse and wearing finely fringed and decorated buckskin trousers and jackets to getting down and mucking about in the creek beds with a gold pan, so it was something of an unusual event that he and I were working together that day. I was resting in the shade of a tall fir tree after spending a couple of fruitless hours digging and panning when I heard Joe holler out from just up the creek, "Praise the Lord Almighty in Heaven! In His infinite MERCY, we have struck it rich today!" He had come up out of the creek bed. and was dancing in circles and gesturing to the heavens in a display of pure joy.

I walked over to him and saw he was not exaggerating. His pan held a good assortment of black sand, small gravel, some easily visible gold grains and a half dozen nuggets as big as pinto beans. We didn't waste any time staking our claims. We each marked our parcels with fir posts at each corner with our names carved in their sides, then we high-tailed it down to Fairplay to record them in the official books.

We were back the next morning, shoveling and panning and slowly filling leather pouches with the yellow metal. That very day, a few hundred other prospectors descended on what they started calling Buckskin Creek, in a tip of their hats to Joe, to stake their own claims. By the end of the week they had already laid out town lots along the creek for the little gold camp they named Laurette, in honor of two of the women, a mother and daughter, in the group. The original name didn't stick, since people kept calling the place Buckskin Joe's Camp and finally just Buckskin Joe. Within a couple of months, Buckskin Joe boasted a population of over two thousand souls, according to the newspaper down in Fairplay, which in truth might have been something of an exaggeration.

Why we refer to ourselves as "souls" like that is a question whose answer has always eluded me. I guess we count cattle by the "head" as if the rest of the carcass is of no account, so maybe there is something to it, like the soul is what really matters and the body, while much easier to count, doesn't matter much.

Like I said, I lost my claim in a poker game not long after that, but I did manage to coax a few hundred dollars in dust and nuggets out of the creek before my night of foolishness. Joe's claim played out pretty fast and it wasn't long before he sold it for a few dollars and lit out for other parts. I have no idea what became of him after that.

After I lost my claim there on Buckskin Creek, I was no longer tied down to a pick, shovel, and gold pan or long-tom, so I was again free to pursue life in the manner I found most agreeable. I could have hired out to other claim-holders as a day laborer, but rambling over the country-side, learning the lay of the land and getting to know the nearby, and farther away, gold camps appealed to me in a way that folks with steady careers in mining, banking or running general stores might not understand. Even though I have called Buckskin Joe my home these past fifty-plus years, I imagine I have spent more nights away from here than I have sleeping in my own loft there above the rafters. Wandering seems to be in my nature. I remember being fascinated by our long trek across the Great Plains. I never tired of the endless movement even when my parents grew weary of the monotony and my little sister complained of sore feet and the frightful size of the prairie.

Despite my early exit from the Buckskin Joe mining business, I could see the placer strike would take a while to play out. It wasn't long before the Phillips Lode and other ore veins were found in the mountains above the creek, so I figured Buckskin Joe would be a going mining camp for at least a year or two, if not a lot longer. So, I set myself up in business as a carpenter and purveyor of fine wild meats and home-grown vegetables—the vegetables only when I had the inclination to rent a wagon and team for the trip to Bear Creek and back, which wasn't all that often—in service to the mining community. This self-employment fit right into my desire for a footloose existence. I spent a few days a week building cabins, sluice-boxes, taverns, jailhouses, potato crates and whatever else anybody needed made out of wood they were willing to pay somebody else to build. I spent a few days a week, sometimes stretching into week-long or month-long treks, hunting for meat to sell in the gold camps or just wandering because I enjoyed it.

I built my cabin up the sunny side of the gulch a little way downstream of the main camp and I have been living here, with no absence longer than a month or two, ever since the fall of 1859.

Like I stated before, it may not have been my cabin to claim ownership of since 1863, in a purely legal sense, and my removal of the signed-over deed from Red's boot may not have been strictly in accordance with the law even way back then, but we do what we have to do and we keep on living. In any case, losing my claim and then almost losing my cabin to the luck of the draw within the space of a few short years—so, maybe four years is a long time for a lesson to take hold—I have to be shown things more than once, sometimes, before they sink in—straightened up my attitude about gambling and life in general, to a great extent. I can say I have never placed an unwise bet since then.

It was soon after I set myself up in Buckskin Joe that I came across my secret place, a place to which I have never invited a single soul. It is one of the finest spots in Colorado, and to my mind and limited experience, in all the world. By the end of 1859, I expect just about every square foot of the Rockies within four hundred miles of Pikes Peak had been trodden over, gazed up at, or looked down upon by prospectors fanning out from the latest gold strikes and hoping to find their own tickets to wealth beyond calculation.

So, when I found what I call the Mosquito Hot Springs in a narrow gulch tucked deep into the shadow of Mosquito Pass, I was surprised to see no evidence of any previous human presence in the place. I suppose it might have been overlooked by miners because there was no color in the gravel in the creek bed leading up to it, and it might have been overlooked by trappers because the little rivulet of a creek leading into the gulch had too little water to be a likely spot for beavers to build their dams and lodges, and it might have been overlooked by the Indians because they never had any good reason to poke around up there near timberline when there was good hunting and fishing in easier terrain far below.

The place is almost invisible from any reasonably accessible vantage point above it. From the summit of Mosquito Pass one can follow a shallow glacial cirque for a mile or more steeply downhill until it pours off of a sheer cliff that must be over a thousand feet high. Ringed by steep rocks on all sides and hidden in a tight cluster of bristle-cone pines at the base of the cliff, the only evidence of the hot springs to a casual observer would be a thin tendril of steam joining the other mists clinging to the sheltered places on frigid winter mornings or chilly summer evenings when the wind is calm, which it rarely is at such an exposed elevation.

I suppose some fool mountaineer with pitons and ropes and a generous helping of insanity could come down off that cirque and lower himself right into the deepest pool where the sulfurous warm waters rise from a deep crack in the earth, but I can't imagine anyone choosing to do that without knowing what a delightful destination awaited him at the bottom.

Coming at the place from below requires a ten-mile hike from the nearest gold camp, followed by a long climb up the forested slope alongside the little nameless creek bed as it meanders back and forth on the lower reaches and then turns steeply up into a narrow rocky gulch that appears to peter out in a forbidding jumble of boulders and downed trees—an avalanche path in winter and treacherous footing in summer. After a difficult climb over the boulders and over the shoulder of the mountainside, the land levels out a bit as the creek meanders again to the base of the cliff, below the cirque pour-off above the last spruce trees and into the bristlecone forest.

The springs well up into three successively lower pools, each filled with clear blue or green water, the apparent color depending on the time of day and the clouds or lack of clouds in the sky, and the amount of mist rising into the air. Some days the mist has a strong sulfur odor and other days it is thin and sweet and barely noticeable. The pools are deep and lined with smooth mineral deposits which make for slippery footing when I cast off my clothes and tiptoe in for a hot bath more luxurious than the finest offerings at the Stanley Hotel or Brown Palace today.

It was a place I visited often, and still visit from time to time despite my creaky joints and general dislike for personal discomfort in my advancing age, despite the labor and time required to get there. I built a few rock benches around the edge of the deepest pool, and laid stone steps descending to a stone ledge I constructed at the perfect depth for sitting with the water up to my neck. That pool is deep enough and wide enough for swimming a few strokes end to end; the other two pools are three or four feet deep in their deepest spots, but less than face-deep for a long stretch at their downstream ends where smooth sand lines the bottom. Those spots are perfect for soaking tired feet and legs while lying in the shallows watching the sky.

During the first months after I discovered that place, Fred and I hauled in timbers and lumber to build a small stable and hay-shed at the edge of the open meadow by the springs. I built a one-room cabin with a rock foundation and rock walls paralleling each side of the creek between the two lowest pools. I laid down plank flooring between the walls about two feet above the surface of the hot water so the place is naturally heated in the winter and on chilly summer nights. It stays downright hot on sunny summer days with the mineral vapors rising up through the floor. A strong roof with shake shingles has successfully shed snow every winter for almost sixty years now, with only a few repairs needed from time to time. I kept the place stocked with the bare essentials needed for a stay of a few days so I could go up there and relax any time I needed to.

When I lie there on my back in one of the shallow pools the 360-degree panorama I see by looking straight up into the jewel-blue sky has to reveal the most glorious prospect on earth, with fourteen thousand foot peaks ringing the scene, separated by high granite saddles rising well over thirteen thousand feet like theater seats of the gods, with dark shadowy cliff faces frequented by soaring croaking ravens, tall spruce trees down the creek just below timberline, and the somber old bristlecone pines, some alive and green, others just gnarled dead white trunks still standing upright, keeping watch in a semi-circle around the edges of the pools. There is usually a light mist rising into the scene and almost always the shrill chatter of pikas in the rocks.

Just writing about that magical place now, sitting here in my cabin with the bitter wind probing the cracks in the door and the unseen, but still felt, weight of snow on the roof, makes me think about making the trek up to those springs one more time—I know that is the direction I will wander off in when the time comes to leave this place for the last time. I could think of many worse places to go. I might even find very special company there as my flesh decomposes and I return to the soil.

Life was pretty good for me in Buckskin Joe during those early years. I was witness to the birth and growth of a vibrant little town, from the first claim-stakes being driven into the gravel to the quick arrival of miners, builders, speculators, ministers of the Lord, saloons, a fine hotel, whores, freight drivers, an assay office, a couple of livery stables, a bank and all the other trappings of a town that sees nothing but a bright future.

Futures died quickly in mining camps, though, and Buckskin Joe was no exception, although it took some years before the last miners moved on and the last buildings were emptied out and left to crumble back into the mountainsides over many winters of freezing, thawing, fire, avalanches and wind. I've been the last holdout up here on Buckskin Creek for many years now. Alma, down at the mouth of the creek where it feeds into the Platte, is still limping along as a nice watering hole on the road between Fairplay and Breckenridge, but I have this place up the gulch all to myself once the snow flies every fall until the melt is finished in late June. I see hunters and hikers and tourist types from time to time, and I don't mind their company even though I don't seek it out.

It was early fall in 1860 when the High Princess of East Slavania came to live in Buckskin Joe. She arrived to great fanfare in a fine coach pulled by a pair of white horses driven by a small man in a black top-coat and fine beaver hat, sporting a thick red mustache above a cleanly shaven chin. Her coach was clearly custom-built, like a small version of the regular stage-coaches plying the roads between Buckskin Joe and Denver, with finely carved details, real glass windows and smoothly polished red lacquer paint emblazoned with the words "Private Coach" and "High Princess of East Slavania" and "See Royalty on Stage Singing and Dancing" in gilt lettering on the sides and rear.

I happened to be delivering potatoes to the general store when her coach drove up, with a cloud of dust following along from down the gulch, and stopped in front of the

Buckskin Lodge and Saloon, one of the premier establishments in town offering beds, food, drink and entertainment. I stood quietly back in the shadows as a small crowd formed around the coach and the driver jumped down to open the side door. He pulled down a folding step and she emerged from the dark interior like an actress making a grand entrance onto a stage.

The first thing I noticed beneath her fine rustling red petticoats was a nicely turned pair of smooth calves and ankles disappearing into red dancing shoes with shining silver heels. Her dress was sleeveless and strapless, so my eyes naturally took in the tightly laced low neckline accentuating the swelling breasts below a double string of gray pearls adorning her neck. She wore long black gloves that came up above her elbows and a black feather hat with a lace veil covering her face down to the middle of her nose. Glorious locks of jet-black hair flowed from beneath her hat and spilled around her shoulders and down her back.

A low murmur and a few whistles issued from the crowd when she curtsied. Her driver led her by the hand up the side steps leading to the saloon's business office door. I was in agreement with the crowd's assessment that this was no common whore who had come to town on this fine fall day when the golden shimmers of the aspen leaves and the blue of the sky suddenly seemed brighter and more magnificent than they had a short time before.

Despite my general lack of enthusiasm for dance-hall music and the various entertainments offered by ladies of the evening in crowded saloons, I determined at once to be among the first to attend whenever the saloon-keeper announced that this fine lady would be singing and dancing for our titillation and amusement. It was not long before the word on the street was the first show would be that very evening. "Silver-Heels," everyone was already calling her because of her alluring footwear and the cumbersome nature of saying "the High Princess of East Slavania" when nobody knew her Christian name, would be gracing the stage just before midnight.

I walked up the gulch from my cabin into Buckskin Joe by the light of a full moon which sent dancing sparkles across the tumbling creek water and lighted my path all the way into town. The Buckskin Lodge and Saloon stood on a flat meadow a few dozen yards back from the creek on the lower end of Buckskin Joe, so it was the first building I came to that evening near midnight. I saw a dozen or more horses hitched up to the front porch rail and a half dozen miners lounging around on chairs outside the front door nursing bottles and shot glasses. The tin tinkling of the piano accompanied by shouting and laughter from inside held the promise of an exciting evening of drinking, card playing, watching the stage shows and dancing with the "dancing girls," of which the saloon employed quite a stable. I walked into the front room past the inn-keeper's desk and stepped down the five stairs into the barroom and theater. I took a seat at a small table as near as I could get to the stage without being right out front with the growing mob of drunken spectators.

I'd had a hand in constructing the place, it being the first of its kind on the creek—a two-story structure of stud-wall construction with board-and-batten siding, windows with counter-weighted sliding sashes and glass panes, a broad front porch and a shake-shingle roof crowned by an iron weather vane. The top floor held twelve guest rooms, six along each side of a narrow corridor leading from the top of the stairs; stairs inside the building, mind you, for the comfort and privacy of the guests. The bottom floor, with its sunken main room hosting the bar, dance floor and stage, could seat one hundred guests at tables around the perimeter of the dance floor and just below the stage, with standing room at the bar for another two dozen.

Sam Bridgeman had built a water-powered sawmill down near Fairplay not long after the gold rush began. He and I had cut the timber and planed the studs and boards for the whole building over a space of about two weeks. Even though I was barely eighteen at the time, Sam put me in charge of the construction crew. We raised the building in about five days, working hours even longer than the miners sluicing gold nuggets out of the creek. It took more than a year for the window glazing to arrive, but the place went into business right after we nailed the last shingle on the roof.

Tessie, one of the few girls I knew by name, since I rarely came into the place, but knew from seeing her around town on several occasions, came from around the bar and made her way through the crowd to my table. "Hi, Jed," she said, half-shouting so her voice rose above the din, "I'm tending bar and waiting tables tonight so Brett can manage the show. What can I get you?"

"Whiskey," I said. I grinned awkwardly up at her. I watched her green dress swish back and forth in rhythm to her hips as she threaded her way back to the bar to fill my order. She was back soon with a bottle of fine whiskey imported from the high desert near Taos—"Taos Lightning"—and a short clear glass which invited filling.

I sipped my whiskey and watched miners and drifters playing cards or dancing with the girls for about five minutes before Brett Smith slipped out onto the front of the stage between the curtains. He motioned to the piano player to stop the music, then he called out, "Ladies and gentlemen, I welcome you to our fine establishment and encourage you to partake liberally of all the diversions we have to offer after the show, but for now I ask you to take your seats."

There was a general shuffling and scraping around the large room as everyone found a chair to sit in or a bar or wall to lean against, then Brett continued, "I am pleased to announce this evening that the Buckskin Lodge and Saloon has negotiated an exclusive arrangement for the enjoyment of the good citizens of Buckskin Joe. For the next six months, every Wednesday and Friday evening until the end of March, or even longer if we are so lucky as to have snow deep enough to keep her here, we have the honor of presenting, on our stage and nowhere else, the talents of the High Princess of East Slavania herself, Miss Ivanalita Slovanofskaya!"

All of the miners, drifters, store clerks, and card sharps in the room erupted into cheers and a stomping of boots on the pine floor I'm sure could be heard halfway to Alma as the curtains parted, the piano burst into life and Miss Ivanalita Slovanofskaya waltzed to center stage and curtsied.

I instantly recognized her by the flashing gray eyes that had been hidden beneath the veil earlier in the day when she stepped down from her coach. Emma Cooper was stunning up there on the stage as she danced and kicked her legs, revealing a good eighteen inches of bare flesh between her bright red skirts and silver-heeled dancing shoes. She sang and danced and cracked jokes in a thick European accent for a solid hour as the entire audience laughed and clapped. The men all leaned forward secretly hoping to get a better look up her skirts or down the front of her low-cut gown.

I sat there in the darkness below the stage drinking in the sight of her, feeling a little confused and uncomfortable. Many of my thoughts out on the prairie and wandering in the mountains had centered around Emma Cooper and how badly I missed her and how I wished we could have known each other better, even though she had never paid me much mind. Of course, the memory I held of her was of a plain farm girl, albeit with rare pretensions to fame and glory, not a saucy dance-hall girl on a barroom stage. Now, here she was two years later, more beautiful and alluring than ever in her stage finery and delicately painted face, and living under a false name. When her show ended and she was bowing to thunderous applause, I slipped away from my table and back down the creek to my cabin.

The name "Silverheels" stuck—nobody even tried to remember her East Slavanian name or call her by it, and I suppose most of the good citizens of Buckskin Joe took her European manner and accent with a grain of salt, anyway. But, her show was a great success. Brett Smith was a happy man, even though rumors circulated she had cut a deal with him that gave her a full fifty percent of the saloon's receipts on the evenings of her engagements, a deal unheard of for any common dance-hall girl. Clearly, Silverheels was special, and she performed to a packed house two nights a week.

What she did during the remainder of her time in Buckskin Joe was something of a mystery to the general public, but part of it in her first few weeks there involved supervising construction of her own three-room house just down the creek from mine. Sam Bridgeman got the contract for the lumber and construction, so it was logical for me to be the foreman of his crew. She came out to the site several times during the weeks it took us to get the house built. She would sit and talk with Sam, smiling and laughing and spewing that thick accent of hers around—I think he was half in love with her by the end of the first day, but then everybody in Buckskin Joe came under her spell before many weeks were out. I managed to avoid any contact with her. My still being shy and awkward around beautiful women was a big part of the reason, but it was also because I wanted to preserve her secrets, whatever they might have been.

So, I was quite surprised to open the door to my cabin on the day we drove the last nail into her roof and find her sitting in my chair warming her hands over my still-warm cook stove.

"Hello, Jedediah P. Carpenter," she said, without the pretense of a foreign accent—it was a fascinating thing to me that she rarely spoke without that accent to anybody except me the whole time she was in Buckskin Joe; she could ease in and out of it just like somebody who had grown up speaking Spanish and English in the same household. She smiled at me with those astonishing gray eyes and a light upturn of her lips, then continued, "It took me a full three minutes to recognize you out there building my house, Buster. I saw you eyeing me when you thought I wasn't paying attention. You aren't sixteen any more, but you haven't changed much. And, considering how easy it was for me to surprise you here, you don't seem any better at covering your backside than you were back there in Nebraska when Clint Williams was trying to teach you a thing or two about not dying young. So, why are you ignoring me?"

I'm sure I blushed at her rebuke, then gave her a sheepish grin and took off my hat. The truth is I had changed a lot over the previous two years. I had not grown an inch, but my shoulders were wider, my arms were stronger, I had a cold piercing stare when I needed to use it, and I had a scraggly beard covering the lower fourth of my face. But, I was still tongue-tied trying to talk to Emma Cooper.

"Pardon my lack of manners, Miss Slovanofskaya," I stammered as I tried to make light use of her alias, "but I didn't figure it would suit your plans for me to let on that the last time I saw you, you were wearing plain prairie clothes and driving a team of oxen into the sunrise, trying to get as far east of me and everything west of St. Louis as you could just as fast as you could."

She laughed and said, "Thank you for your caution."

I was thrilled to be back in Emma's presence. I wanted to know all about where she had been and how she had gotten all the way back here to Buckskin Joe. But, she cut our conversation short by saying, "I need to move along before tongues start wagging about you and me being inside your house alone. A working girl has her reputation to think of, after all. Maybe we can talk after my show some time." She smiled at me again, then said, "And, Jed, thank you for trying to talk me out of leaving with Zeke Jones. You and Clint were right about him. I hope I never have to see his face again on this side of Hell."

Her coarse language surprised me, but not much. She nodded to me as she went out my door to organize moving her things into her new house.

She did manage to maintain a positive reputation, of sorts, during those months in Buckskin Joe. While most of the dancing girls at the saloons around town would take any man with a few grains of gold dust back to the cribs for a toss in the hay, Silverheels came to be known as a high-class woman with very particular tastes. She kept the best room upstairs at the Buckskin Lodge for entertaining her gentleman friends, and her assignations were as rare as they were discreet. Rumors circulated that her going rate was never less than twenty five dollars, which was quite a sum in those days, and even then she only accepted invitations from men who matched her standards, which definitely did not allow for dalliances with the common run of prospectors and card dealers who frequented the saloon. I never even considered offering her my commerce, since I thought she still saw me as the awkward sixteen year old who helped her bury her parents out there on the Nebraska prairie that hot summer day.

But, we became friends. I tried to make it my business to be around at the end of most of her shows. She would come out after the curtain fell to find me at my table tucked away in the shadows along the wall farthest from the bar and dance floor.

The first evening she came out from backstage to sit with me, there were jeers and catcalls and sly winks from the rabble aimed my direction, but it didn't take many nights before our routine became accepted as normal. I think everybody thought we were friends like a brother and sister, and I had a reputation for a slow fuse on my temper, but a violent explosive side for anyone who persisted in lighting the fuse and encouraging it to burn—particularly after an incident with the Bradley boys down in Fairplay that left one of them unconscious and the other wishing he was—maybe I will have time to relate that story somewhere in the following pages, or maybe not—so we were left alone in the half-lit barroom to converse at will.

I sat across from her, nursing a drink and tapping my left foot on the floor—a habit I noticed came around any time I was nervous about something. She had changed out of her fancy stage clothes and wore a long-sleeved dress buttoned up to her collarbone. Her hair was piled into a tight bun on the back of her head. Tiny drops of perspiration dotted her face as she cooled down from the excitement and exertion of performing. Her eyes looked tired and a little sad. This is not to say she was not still stunningly beautiful, which she most definitely was.

We talked about inconsequential things for a few minutes, until we were no longer drawing the attention of the people around us. Then her voice dropped into a quieter tone without the strain of a put-on foreign accent.

"I saw Clint Williams a while back on his little farm down there on Bear Creek. I would not have thought of him as the type to stay put anywhere for long, but he seemed right satisfied. He surprised me when he said you were living out here near Fairplay. I thought you had your mind set on Oregon," she commented, taking a sip of my whiskey.

"I was," I replied, "but the Good Lord directed me otherwise. A lightning strike, two dead oxen, and help from Clint's 'goddam Indian'—one of the best friends I have ever had, he's turned out to be—set me off in this direction. I don't expect to leave these parts any time soon, either."

I filled in some of the details of my life during the two years since we had parted, then I asked her about herself. She seemed unwilling to tell me everything she had done since 1858, but I picked up on hints and inferences from this and later conversations that gave me a pretty good picture of how things had been. Of course, after all these years I don't remember her exact words, but this is about how her story unfolded over the next several weeks:

"I know I put on a big show of worldliness and independence out there on the prairie," she said, "but the truth is I was scared half out of my mind and didn't know what to do. I saw Zeke Jones as a way to get back east to a world I knew a little more about, and I was too proud to let you and Clint talk me out of going with him."

"I was a fool to think I could trust Zeke, but that morning when I went out to make the deal with him to take me back east, he was all smiles and charm and he promised me everything I asked him for. He was helpful and acted like a true gentleman all the first day as we headed east, but the farther east we got, the more he showed his true colors. He beat his horse when it stumbled climbing up a steep gully and he cursed his drivers whenever he thought we were moving too slow. He started drinking the next morning and started leering at me and making suggestions I had never heard from any man before. By then, I was sure I had made a big mistake, but I couldn't see any way around my situation.

"I thought I knew something about how to handle men and keep myself safe, but I was just a foolish girl who didn't know anything. I used to tease and flirt around all the men I knew, which wasn't all that many where we lived back in Missouri. They all knew me and my folks and I can see now none of them would have hurt me for anything in the world.

"Zeke and his men were different. I fought back like a she-bear at first, but Zeke's fists quickly put a stop to that. And there were four of them and only one of me." She kept her eyes lowered towards the table between us as she told me this, only glancing up after a long pause.

"By the time we got to St. Louis, Zeke had sold off everything I owned except the clothes in my trunk. He even sold my books, which meant a lot more to me than most of the other stuff in my wagon. I love to read about places all over the world and dream about seeing them and singing for the people there. One of my favorite books was a finely illustrated one about India and the Hindu gods and goddesses my mother gave me, which I think I had read thirty times or more. I never saw a dime of the money he got from any of my things. He kept Star of Midnight for himself, too, just like he said he might.

"He put me to work in the cribs along the waterfront and —I don't know why I'm telling you any of this, Jed, but somehow I think I can trust you and you might understand— he beat me black and blue more than once when he thought I wasn't working hard enough or when he thought I might be holding back on giving him all the money I earned .

"Well, it wasn't long before I was a girl in real trouble. Zeke got even meaner with me then and made me keep working right up until the end. I don't remember much about the last few weeks before I got away from him. Laudanum took away the pain and the memories, too. I think there was a fat nurse with cold hands and a doctor with smelly breath and an evil leer, and I am almost certain they said it was a girl before they took it away, but my mind might be playing tricks on me. I know there was a lot of blood and dirty sheets, and a day or two of doing nothing but sleeping before Zeke came around to take me away."

I was dumbstruck by her story and wasn't saying anything, just looking at her with what I hoped was an understanding aspect. I found it hard to take in how she could have survived such horrible events relatively unscathed —she seemed so poised and self-confident up there on the stage, and she seemed so calm talking to me—but I suspected if I scratched very hard beneath her calm outer shell I would find a torrent of anger and hate and suffering she had to work hard to keep a lid on. She took another sip of my drink and set the glass down. I pushed it across the table and gestured that it was hers to finish.

"Thanks," she said. She downed it in about three gulps, then she looked me straight in the eyes and held my gaze. There was a hard edge to her stare I had not seen up until then.

"Somewhere in the middle of all that pain and the stupor from the drugs, I determined I would never again let my life be controlled by anybody but me, especially not a man like Zeke Jones. Somewhere along the way back from the doctor's place to Zeke's hotel, I balled up my courage and hit him square in the face with his ivory-topped cane. He shrieked like a little girl and I saw blood streaming down his face as I jumped from his coach and took off into the night.

"'Emma Cooper!' he screamed—I'll never forget his shrill voice when he screamed like that—'Emma Cooper, you can't get away from me!'—he was still screaming when I rounded a corner and disappeared down an alley close to the river.

"I knew I might get murdered by thieves or drunks in that alley, but I figured if I stayed with Zeke he would kill me sooner or later anyway, so I didn't care about what was in front of me. I just wanted to get away from Zeke Jones, and, as of this evening, at least, I have been successful in that endeavor."

She paused and looked around the dark room for a few seconds before continuing, "He followed me from St. Louis to Chicago, but I slipped away from him. Then he almost caught me in Cleveland before I started using a different name and came back west. He claims I took something from him and he wants it back. I don't know what that might be, beyond my body, mind and soul. I swear I think the man is a lunatic. I hope he is really stupid and thinks because I was heading further east the last two times he found me I will be in New York or Paris by now."

She smiled, a tight little smile that betrayed little real joy, then waited for me to carry the conversation for a while. Tres-Bien, the Lodge's resident mouser cat, appeared from the shadows and hopped into Emma's lap. She stroked his sleek black fur tears welled up in the corners of her eyes. The cat settled into licking his white paws with his pink tongue.

"Well, Emma," I said after a long pause, "I'm sure sorry things turned out like that for you."

"You must think very badly of me," she cast her eyes down and wouldn't hold my gaze.

"No," I said, "I don't think badly of you at all. This is a harsh world and we all do what we have to do."

"Thank you for that," she said.

I shifted in my seat and leaned forward, speaking in a low voice. "One thing I can say, though, if I ever find Zeke Jones sniffing around west of Omaha, his remaining days will be painful and numbered in single digits."

"Oh, no, Jed, you mustn't think like that. I despise Zeke Jones and will gladly greet him in Hell, but you must promise me you will not try to kill him if he turns up around here. That man is evil to the core and he wouldn't hesitate to squash you like a cricket." She pleaded with her gray eyes as she said this.

So, I promised her I would not kill Zeke Jones, which is a promise I can honestly say I have kept.

"So, how did you end up in Buckskin Joe?" I asked out of curiosity, but also to direct the conversation away from the subject of Zeke Jones.

She giggled and a real glint of joy returned to her eyes. "Did you notice my driver?"

"Yeah, short guy with a big mustache?"

"Yes. His name is Dirk Travers. He's just about the shrewdest business man I have ever met. Do you know what he did with that fancy coach that was all painted up with that "High Princess" malarkey the night of my first show after all the saloons closed down?"

"I have no idea."

"He drove it out of town in the dark of night and took it back to Denver. Before two more days went by it would have been repainted to say "Royal Duchess of Brittany" on the sides and he would have been halfway to some other mining camp with another girl like me. That's what he's been doing since the California gold rush—he has a whole stable of girls he takes out to the mining camps in the fall before the first snow starts. He knows most of the miners hole up for the winter and don't leave their camps because they're afraid of claim jumpers, and he knows after the ground freezes solid there's not much for them to do but drink whiskey and spend money on fancy ladies. By the time Buckskin Joe is frozen in for the winter, all these old prospectors around here will gladly pay a goodly sum to see my show two nights a week. Isn't that just the most brilliant idea? Before winter sets in Dirk will have girls set up all over the gold fields, taking money from cabin-fever-crazed old goats like all these men in here who will have nothing to do with their time but spend money!

"It's not just girls for the winter, either. He has about ten of us he takes around to the real booming gold camps—the cream of the crop, he calls us—, but he has a lot more girls he sets up every summer for a couple of months in little places all over the territory. I guess some of them are spinster school-teachers looking for a little excitement during the summer farming season when they are out of work. Some of them sing and dance, but most of them are just getting by on their looks and their willingness to do things for money most women would never consider doing at all. I bet the good ones make more money in one summer in those little gold camps than they do in ten years of teaching back in Kansas."

I saw the cleverness of the plan and had to admire this Dirk Travers for putting it into motion. But, I generally do not expect fair dealing from anyone, especially not someone who trades in the various talents of beautiful women. I had to ask Emma, "So what's in it for you?"

She narrowed her eyes and thought for a moment before answering. "Jed, I believe Dirk Travers is one of the decent men of the world, of which I have to say there are not many. I've traveled with him all the way from Kansas City and he has not once caused me any sort of discomfort. Some of the girls have worked with him more than ten years, so that should tell you something about him. And, his business deal with us is very fair. He gives us half of everything he gets from the deals he makes, and we give him half of everything we might make in whatever other money-making enterprises we may engage in."

I raised my eyebrows and commented, "Well, I can't imagine what any of those activities might entail. Double-jack mining, or hauling explosives, maybe?" I was trying to be half funny, but deeper down I was trying to cover up my anger and jealousy over the images I saw of what she might do in her off hours to make extra money.

She pouted a little at that and then said, "Maybe it's time for you to mind your own business, Buster." Dark clouds gathered inside her gray eyes and knew I was treading dangerously close to the edge of a place she did not want to delve into any further.

I steered away from any discussion of what she and the other girls might do on the side for extra money by gazing around the saloon without saying anything for a minute or two. Then, I did some figuring and said, "Well, if I have the picture in my mind right, this Dirk fellow is paying his girls half of what he takes in for getting them set up on stages and dance floors across the land. In return, they give him half of everything they make over and above the official deal. So, let's say he has thirty girls working for him, between the ten you say he places every winter and maybe another twenty who only work for him in the summer. Hmm, that works out to him raking in the entire income of maybe fifteen working ladies providing entertainment for bored men in the world's richest mining camps. Brilliant, he definitely is."

The conversation lagged at that point, so we called it a night about the time the saloon closed its doors.

It was around this time I became friends with the Reverend John Dyer—his followers called him "Father Dyer" in later years—over the course of my various travels between Denver and Bear Creek and Fairplay and Buckskin Joe. Reverend Dyer was one of those few decent men in the world Emma referred to. He was a Methodist circuit rider by calling, but the Lord's work didn't pay very well in those days, so he turned his hand to just about anything that would pay him a few dollars here and there: court clerking, contract mail hauling, ore transport, and even some carpentry which he joined me in on more than one occasion. He was in his late forties then, which I considered inconceivably old at that time in my raw youth, but I quickly learned he could outwork me and anybody else half his age and still have energy left over for preaching to anybody who cared to listen.

I remember one Sunday morning he rode into Buckskin Joe and talked Brett Smith into letting him turn the Buckskin Lodge and Saloon into a church meeting house for the morning. He went out on the street and rang the big bell over the saloon door, then he leaned back and hollered up and down for everybody who was awake and about, and maybe even those who were still in bed nursing hangovers, to come around to the saloon at ten o'clock. "There'll be preachin' and singin', so come on in!" he yelled.

Well, I was surprised to see the crowd that turned out. Must have been three dozen people there, between the single men and the few citizens who had wives and children with them—wives and children who would under no circumstances have ever darkened the door of that particular establishment before that morning—and passing travelers from the rented rooms above the barroom. There were even a few of the saloon girls who came and went during the morning and early afternoon. And there was preaching and singing to last most of the day, except for the short break we took around noon for a potluck dinner, until about an hour before sundown when it became clear new arrivals were there waiting for the bar to open back up again. It was along about then that Brett encouraged the good reverend to move along to the benediction.

Reverend Dyer and I had traveled the roads together a few times before, so I invited him to stay at my place for the night. I fixed him up a bedroll over in the corner beyond the stove and we sat and talked in the growing darkness until I could see we would need to light the lamp if we wanted to keep talking. I invited Emma over from next door and we all shared a light supper of biscuits and venison stew.

Emma always dressed in plain clothes and did not put on her fake accent when she was a guest in my house among a few select friends, which was not as often as I would have enjoyed, so it took a while for the preacher to figure out who she was. I think he must have thought she was a spinster school teacher or a store clerk's daughter before I made some comment about her singing for a living.

"Oh, you're a singer, then?" he asked Emma. I was a little embarrassed at having steered the conversation in this direction. But, one thing Emma never showed was any shame over her profession.

She answered him without elaboration, "Yes, the boys around here call me 'Silverheels'."

When the truth of her occupation dawned upon him, I was afraid he might admonish her and try to dissuade her from her evil ways, but his response was warm and welcoming.

"My dear girl, I thought you were too pretty to be single and living in these parts. But, now I understand. It's not for me to judge your livelihood. I would be honored to hear you sing sometime. We are all called by the Lord to do His work, and I have absolute faith you will find ways to glorify Him in this earthly realm." So, thanks to his humility and Emma's general radiance, I was perfectly comfortable sharing my table with the two of them, which we managed to do three or four more times before our lives came unraveled in ways none of us ever expected.

Besides his work for the Lord, John Dyer is probably best remembered for his midnight treks over Mosquito Pass in the dead of winter carrying the mail between Fairplay and Leadville. I joined him on one of his mail runs when I decided to go over into the headwaters of the Arkansas River scouting for good hunting places. We left Fairplay about eleven o'clock one evening, since Reverend Dyer wanted to traverse the deep snow up and down the pass in the deepest hours of the night so the crust on top would be frozen solid and there would be no melting from warm sunlight to trigger avalanches.

We strapped long boards to our boots—"snowshoes", he called them—that let us clump sideways up the steep drifts and slide down their backsides at speeds I found terrifying on more than one occasion. He showed me how to carry a water-skin inside my coat to keep it from freezing and what kinds of food to take for the trip to give us the energy we needed to travel without stopping for more than very short breaks.

It must have been sometime around three in the morning when we came upon a fellow traveler who was frozen stiff, his legs sticking up out of a bowl of heavily perturbed snow and his head buried beneath the surface. We grabbed him by the feet and pulled him up onto the trail. I turned him over and brushed the snow off of his face, but I didn't recognize him.

"I've seen this more than once up here on the back side of the pass," Reverend Dyer said. "These young fellas come up here not knowing what they're about, loaded down with a pack they can barely carry. Then, they get tired and wobbly or just don't pay attention and step off the hard-packed snow in the middle of the trail and fall off into deep powder that stays shaded by the trees. Those drifts might be twelve feet deep this time of year, and you can't hardly struggle back out of them once you fall in."

I think if I had been alone on that trip, I might have made the same mistake as our poor dead friend. In any case, it would have taken me a good three days broken up by freezing nights huddled in snow caves to make the trip on my own, but that old man slogged up and down Mosquito Pass, over thirteen thousand feet high, and covered the forty some-odd miles between Fairplay and Leadville in about twelve hours.

My friendship with him showed me a thing or two about age, and a thing or two about what it means to be a truly decent man, but the good reverend never managed to convince me of the Truth of his particular brand of theology. We had many long discussions about the nature of the Lord when we shared conversation over the dying embers of campfires when we happened to be traveling the same roads from wherever we had come from to wherever we were going.

I knew from my extensive reading that the sharpest minds in the history of humanity, from the earliest literate Greeks right down to the founders of the United States of America, had never been able to agree on the true nature of God, or even to agree on the simple existence of a God, so I was in no hurry to come to any conclusions on my own. My mother was a Quaker and my father never talked much about religion. She never told me what to believe, but frequently encouraged me to read the Bible and to sit quietly, wherever I was, listening for the whisper of the Holy Spirit. I have done what she said many times over the years, and the whispers I hear are full of beauty and grace and terror, but they never impart any details I can form any kind of explainable theology around.

I hear people talk about taking the "Leap of Faith" all the time, like taking the opinion of the Apostle Paul and making it their own, in the absence of any supporting evidence, would somehow make them more acceptable in the eyes of the Lord. Well, I have done my own wandering in the wilderness and I am not blind to the glories of Creation, but nothing I have experienced myself says anything about Original Sin or being Saved by the Christ or any other theological nonsense. The Lord may be my Shepherd, but I can tell you right now I have survived to my current old age by watching my own backside—it took me a good many years and a great deal of God-given luck before I learned to do this well—and carrying finely crafted weapons. I consider the existence of a God who is active in the affairs of men to be an open question, with the idea of a Deity who started the world spinning and then wandered off leaving it to run on its own making a lot more sense.

In those early days in the Colorado gold camps, justice came at the hands of those on hand to administer it. As far west as the Arkansas River, the land was still technically a part of Kansas Territory, but the long arms of administrative rule were weak and palsied by the time they reached all the way west as far as places like Buckskin Joe. It was a couple of years before the Congress wised up and conjured Colorado Territory into being. In the meantime, the first prospectors to stake claims in any new gold strike would organize themselves into their own governing body, creating rules of fair play (thus the name of Fairplay, after some of the early times in gold camps preceding it did not reflect much in the way of fair play or justice for anybody beyond the initial claimants) for claim sizes, town-lot platting, rules of behavior and other necessities of a civilized community.

In large part, this spontaneous exercise of democracy and the rule of law was an effective way to build the Territory, from the grass roots (or placer gravel, as it were) up. But there were problems, at times, that made men like me a little suspicious of the justness of the justice that might be meted out in some circumstances, especially when local big-shots were involved or when the blood of the mob was stirred up like a hornet's nest. So, we would, if the nature of the situation dictated its propriety, take the law into our own hands, from time to time.

A case in point was the time in Fairplay when the presiding judge at the courthouse ruled a clearly guilty man innocent of the murder he had committed. The mob suspected money had changed hands in the judge's chambers before the verdict was handed down. In that instance, the good people of the little city removed the murderer from the jailhouse and administered their own punishment, after which they left a length of rope with frayed threads at one end and a tightly coiled noose at the other end lying on the judge's desk.

Then there was the time Reverend Dyer was riding into town and encountered a man fleeing for his life in advance of an approaching lynch-mob. The good reverend made quick inquiries of the man before deciding to give him sanctuary on the back of his horse until he could quiet the mob and sort things out peacefully, the result being the fleeing man was found to have been wrongly accused and was immediately set free.

Here I am again, drifting away from the main thread of my story. It's time to poke at the embers in the stove and add some wood to the firebox so I can heat up my dinner, then I will retire with a good bottle of Tennessee sipping whiskey and return to this Testimony in the early hours tomorrow morning. The moon is just a few days short of being full, so I might strap on my own snow-shoes tonight and go out for a quiet stroll up and down the creek. The crisp air—I expect it is about ten degrees below zero outside—would do my lungs good, and the moonlight on the snow-drifts will make it like daylight outside. If I'm lucky, I might hear wolves crying in the night, but at the very least I will hear the shooshing of my own feet moving through the snow.

I kept my promise to Emma about not killing Zeke Jones one week in late September of 1860, after she had been in Buckskin Joe for less than a month. And in the process of not killing Zeke, I got her horse back for her, too. I had ridden Fred down towards South Park and happened upon John Dyer walking beside the road a few miles down the river from Alma. I paused and offered him a ride, which he gladly accepted by climbing up behind me. Fred didn't put in a word of protest about the extra weight on his back. Despite the reputation mules have acquired, Fred was generally agreeable to most anything I asked of him.

I found out the good reverend was heading down to Denver with a full mail pouch. I told him I was headed out into the prairie lands in South Park to do some hunting and offered to give him a ride as far as Como. We were still a good distance from Fairplay when I happened to glance off into a meadow that reached across the South Platte and up into the timber's edge where the ground rose up the mountainside. I saw what looked to be a solid black horse hobbled in the grass near the trees. It was not unusual for travelers to stop along the river to hobble their horses in meadows like this one so they could eat their fill while their riders rested or camped for a night or two before they hit the trail again. So, I noted the scene and kept Fred pointed down the road. Something about that horse kept niggling at me, so after about five minutes I found a good ford and led Fred and Reverend Dyer and myself across the river and back upstream.

As we approached the horse, I saw it was a mare, not solid black but sporting a bright white blaze on her chest. Drawing closer, I saw the "SC" brand on her rump.

I leaned back around towards Reverend Dyer and whispered, "That horse belongs to Emma Cooper. Whoever rode her into this territory is no friend of Emma's, so let's watch and listen and keep what we know to ourselves." His brow furrowed with concern, but he nodded his understanding and assent. We both dismounted. I took my bow, quiver of arrows and bedroll off of Fred's back and let him browse in a patch of low chokecherries near the riverbank. Reverend Dyer and I sat on a downed tree-trunk by the river and proceeded to share a meal of hard cheese and bread and to engage in aimless conversation while we both kept our eyes and ears open.

We sat there for several minutes and saw no sign of any human presence other than Star of Midnight grazing across the meadow. I formulated a plan in my mind while we sat.

"I tell you what, Reverend," I said. "It's a long way to Denver, and I would like to save you from that long walk by letting you have Fred's services from this point on your journey. Take good care of him and bring him back around to Buckskin Joe whenever you happen to be back up this way."

Reverend Dyer gave me a long look and then said, "Jed, that's a generous offer, but I'm concerned about how you'll carry on with your hunting plans if I take you up on it."

"I'm going to cut my hunt short and return that fine black mare to its rightful owner," I said, "since there doesn't seem to be anybody around to make any contrary ownership claims."

"Maybe you should tell me a little more about that horse and how Emma came to lose her," Reverend Dyer said.

I felt like I owed him a fuller explanation, but I didn't want to burden his thoughts with any more of Emma's story than he already knew. And, I expected he would not let me act on my own if he knew what was really on my mind. So, I just said, "That may be fodder for story-telling around a warm fire one of these upcoming long winter nights, but for now, I think I need to keep the details to myself. I will just say the last time I saw that horse, I was trying to talk Emma out of going back East with the man who ended up stealing it from her. If he is the one who rode that mare into South Park, the only reason he would be out here is to find Emma again. It will not be an easy time for Emma if he does find her, and I intend to see that will never happen."

"Well," he said, "I appreciate the offer and I will take excellent care of your fine mule between now and when we see each other again. Just remember the Lord works in ways we may not understand, so do not take it upon yourself to interfere with his Plan or to make Judgments on his behalf."

"I assure you I will not," I replied. I helped him get back on Fred's back and watched him ford the river and get back on the road towards Fairplay. I had now made two promises concerning my future behavior regarding Zeke Jones, and I am happy to say I managed to keep both of them.

I left my bedroll in a small clearing just inside the edge of the woods near the meadow where Star of Midnight was grazing. Carrying only my bow and quiver, I started making widening circles around her until the signs I cut gave me a good indication of the direction her rider had gone off in on foot. There was a clear trail of boot prints in the mud and broken branches to follow into the woods across a flat area that ran parallel to a wide bend in the river that took it a good half mile away from the more direct line of the stage road between Alma and Fairplay.

That is truly glorious country-side, with low shrubs and rich grasses filling the flat along the river and multiple large ponds up side creeks made by beavers in decades past. Across the narrow valley to the east is a high mountain standing out alone overlooking Alma and Fairplay, and even higher mountains rising to the west, their spruce and fir-covered slopes coming right down to the edge of the Middle Fork of the South Platte River. At certain places along the river, the view upward takes in ridges and peaks jutting several thousand feet above the tree-line, capped in deep white snow for nine or ten months every year. From that place along the river, it is just a few more miles downstream where the broad expanse of South Park widens out like an ocean of grass and low hills pouring from a funnel.

The trail I followed veered out to the riverbank several times before moving back into the easier terrain going through the trees. It crossed back and forth across the river a time or two at shallow places that were easy to ford. At each spot along the riverbank the boot prints told a story of a man stopping to fish, or to gaze upward at the sky or the mountains, apparently not in a particular hurry to keep moving. The size and depth of the boot prints also told me it was more likely than not that they belonged to a man much larger than average, a man like Zeke Jones. I approached each turn towards the river taking care to keep behind brush or trees so I would see first rather than being seen first. I was an excellent hunter and could stalk my prey soundlessly and with focused awareness. It was during times I was not hunting that I could be unaware of my surroundings and likely to be taken by surprise, as Clint Williams and Emma Cooper were so fond of pointing out to me.

The last time the trail of prints turned from the woods in towards the river was along a small creek running into the river from the east, across from a wide canyon and creek feeding in from the other side on the west. A cluster of spindly aspen trees at the bottom of the opposite slope indicated the area had been disturbed at some time in the not-too-distant past, since aspens move in to take over land left by spruce and fir trees when they burn or are taken down by avalanches and landslides. When I crept close enough to see the river through the brush, I saw the aspens were growing up through a fresh pile of rocks and debris from an avalanche path scarring the mountainside. The rocks had clattered down the mountain all the way across the riverbed, which was running in a roaring rapid over the boulders and buried spruce logs trying to block its path and backing up a good-sized pond behind them.

I smelled the mouthwatering aroma of freshly-cooked trout before I saw blue wisps of smoke rising from behind the thick brush lining the riverbank. About the same time, I heard human moaning and cursing and splashing water. Slipping along a narrow game trail dotted with fresh deer and raccoon tracks, I soon reached a vantage point in the brush that let me see along the river's edge.

First, I saw a wooden rack holding gutted trout butterflied open over a small fire with smoking embers in a ring of stones. Then, I saw a man's legs protruding up the wet gravel behind a large boulder sunk in the riverbed where it blocked the rest of my view. The legs thrashed against the wet gravel amid moans and shrieks varying in message from low determination to mid-level anguish to rising panic. I nocked an arrow onto my bowstring and emerged from the brush to get a look around the boulder.

There I saw Zeke Jones. I hadn't seen him in more than two years, but I was certain it was him. The form sprawled out on its belly, half in and half out of the water, was well over six feet long and almost as wide and ended in a head adorned with long black hair no longer wearing a hat, which was floating in an eddy about ten feet downstream. I looked back and saw Zeke's coat hung over a dead spruce branch, his rifle leaning against a tree and his knife stuck by its point in a log near the fire. Zeke did not see me, so he continued thrashing about in the water and cursing. His right hand and forearm disappeared into deep water beyond a muddy mound that dropped off steeply from the flatter gravel bank. He was clutching at his right arm with his left hand, reaching deep into the water and twisting his face into a pained grimace as he worked away at something that was invisible to me in the mud-clouded water.

I stood quietly for a few seconds to wait for Zeke's latest linguistic tirade to fade, then asked, "Having some trouble, there, mister?"

Zeke roared "YES," in a mixture of relief and frustration as he tried to turn over to look at me. He drew his legs up by propping up on his left hand and taking short alternating steps until he crabbed around into the river and stood upright in the deep water facing me. His right hand was still down in the water, so he had to lean over like a green willow branch as he did this. His thick black beard was dripping water back into the river.

"God damn beaver trap!" he yelled, almost like he blamed me and not the trap for his predicament.

The picture became clear to me then. The trap must have been forgotten many years before, since there had not been much active trapping in this vicinity during the short years I had been here. It would have been set right in the edge of the water, buried in shallow mud at the bottom of a beaver run, perched just on the lip of a steep drop-off into deeper water. The trap would have been anchored to the riverbed by a chain which would drag a trapped animal into deep enough water to drown as it struggled to free itself.

The trap had lain there in shallow mud for years, forgotten or abandoned by the trappers who placed it there, jaws set open and waiting for its intended victim. In this case, the victim was Zeke Jones, who was minding his own business smoking some trout when he decided to wash the fish guts and slime off of his hands in the clear calm cold inviting water at the edge of the river.

"I see you are in a real jam," I said. "Steel jaws on a soft hand in freezing water can't be a Sunday picnic, sir, I can readily see that." I sat back on my haunches, relaxed my grip on my bow, and returned the arrow to its quiver.

Zeke gave me a puzzled look, tinged by the pain in his eyes, and said, "So, are you going to help me? The rocks are too damn slippery to keep a foothold, so my feet are useless. I've dunked myself so many times I've come close to drowning trying to work with my feet and one good hand to get those damn jaws open."

"Well, sir," I observed calmly, I like to think without a trace of irony or vaunting or other puffery in my voice, "it does seem the Lord works in mysterious ways."

"What the hell are you blabbering about, boy? Get down here and help me!"

"No, sir," I said. "I'm afraid I can't do that. I would just kill you outright to put you out of your misery, but there is a lovely lady up in Buckskin Joe—around these parts she's known as 'Silverheels' but I expect you would know her better as Emma Cooper—well, anyway, she made me promise I would never do that. And, as for your current predicament, I promised a good and decent man of the cloth, not more than two hours ago, I would not interfere in the unfolding of God's Plan by taking any action of my own which might call into question His right to judge. So, I think I will just sit here a spell. I might even partake of the pair of trout smoking over yonder embers which smell like they are prepared to perfection about now."

I saw no point in continuing to talk with Zeke, even though I might have taken great pleasure in reminding him who I was and refreshing his memory about our parting words out there on the Nebraska prairie over two years gone. It would have done him no good to continue arguing with me about whether to help him or not, his energy being better spent trying to figure a way out of his mess. So I went over to his fire and enjoyed his trout while he continued to thrash about in the water, pausing at regular intervals to curse me and my family line roundly in colorful terms I need not repeat here. When I finished eating, I strolled back down to the water's edge to rinse my hands, being sure to stay out of Zeke's reach.

"It's nice of the Lord to provide clean wash water after such a fine meal," I said. "You just have to watch out for grizzly bears, leg-hold traps and other hazards when you lean down to rest your paws in places unfamiliar to you." By this time, Zeke had just about worn himself out trying to open the jaws holding his hand under the cold water. His lips were slate-blue and his clothes were thoroughly soaked. I figured he wouldn't last many hours past sundown.

"Well, I'll be moseying along, mister. I wish you well on your journey across the River Styx. Old Charon should be rowing up to collect you any time now. It's kind of a shame, you know? You wouldn't be facing that dark journey into Hades today if you had chosen a different course of action with respect to Emma Cooper out there on the prairie a few years back."

To this day, I have to admit a tiny touch of remorse at these little taunts I threw in Zeke's direction, but I salve my conscience by remembering the things I had considered doing to him, but did not do, ever since that day he rode off into the east following Emma Cooper's wagon.

I gathered my bow and Zeke's things and headed back up the trail towards Star of Midnight. I make no personal claims to virtue or potential saint-hood, so I will readily acknowledge I got good use out of Zeke's rifle over the years —it's the fine Sharps up there on the rack beside the door— and I have cleaned a trout or two of my own catching with his knife, which keeps a very fine edge even in the roughest use. I searched his coat before I threw it into the brush and enriched myself to the tune of one hundred twelve dollars in folding money and coins, along with a finely crafted gold pocket watch.

I mounted Star of Midnight and rode into Fairplay for the night. I engaged in an evening of drinking and card-playing during which I managed to lose over half of my new-found wealth, which was somewhat made up for by the hot bath and good breakfast I enjoyed at the Fairplay Hotel.

In the morning I rode Star of Midnight back up to Buckskin Joe. Along the way, a few miles downstream of Alma, at a wide bend in the river where it meanders away towards the western side of the valley, I noticed a scattering of turkey vultures and ravens gliding in circles above an avalanche chute that ended with its foot down in the river beyond the trees and brush and out of sight of any casual travelers passing by along the stage road.

A good ten years later I saw a brief item in the "Fairplay Citizen" describing the discovery of skeletal remains tangled up in a beaver trap in the river beyond a stand of thick brush a few miles downstream of Alma. "A tragic trapping accident, many years old, victim unknown" was the sheriff's conclusion when he was asked to comment on the case.

The sky had turned a foreboding gun-metal gray and the wind kicked up into a gale before I got to Alma. Snow fell in heavy clumps that soon turned to a steady rush of tiny flakes that piled up in powder six inches deep along the road by the time I got to Buckskin Joe.

I got back into town in the early evening and put Star of Midnight up at the livery stable, prepaid for the first two weeks. I paid the stable hand a dollar to deliver a note to Emma up at the Buckskin Lodge and Saloon. It was one of her show nights and I didn't want to hang around late enough to talk to her.

The note just said, "There is something that belongs to you, free and clear, up at the Livery Stable. — Jed."

I was pretty worn out by my little adventure with Zeke, so I decided to go up to the Mosquito Hot Springs for a few days of rest and reading. Reverend Dyer was probably passing the storm with Fred somewhere between Kenosha Hill and Denver, so I packed up some books and a few days' worth of food, along with my bow, arrows and a thick bedroll, and headed out on my snow-shoes. The snow tapered off and the sky cleared by the time I reached the cutoff from the Mosquito Pass road heading up to my special place. I looked behind me as I climbed in the snow-muffled silence and saw my tracks clearly marked by the moonlight on the fresh snow clinging to the trail.

After most of a night of slipping and sliding on the fresh snow—most of it had melted on the warm autumn-sun-baked rocks as fast as it had fallen, so the ground offered a slippery soup of slush on wet rocks for my boots and snow-shoes to try to grip—up the avalanche chute into the flats below the cirque pour-off, I finally arrived at the springs. Dawn was first tickling the eastern ridge-tops when I arrived, leaving a fading splash of stars across the cold sky. I made my camp, a canvas lean-to strung between two thick tree trunks, my bedroll on soft pine needles I revealed by brushing the thin snow beneath the pine boughs away, preferring to stay out-of-doors in the fresh autumn air rather than staying in the warmer, but less open confines of my stone hut.

I ate a cold breakfast of hard biscuits, then stripped down and slogged in my bare feet to the nearest hot pool, the one that was just deep enough to lie down in, to cover myself in steaming water with my head resting on a flat rock holding my face above the surface. I lay there watching the sky lightening up with the growing dawn, basking in the luxurious hot mineral waters rising up from deep below the mountains. The last visible stars faded away into the deep azure sky ringed by rising warm mists about the time I drifted off into a deep sleep.

"What have I told you about watching your backside, Buster?"

I threw my eyes open wide to see Emma Cooper sitting on the rocks rising out of the pool, her bare feet soaking in the water. She grinned down at my naked body and splashed warm water across the pool towards my face. I sat up quick and covered myself with my hands as best I could there on those bare rocks in water less than a foot deep. My skin was wrinkled all over from my hours-long soak in the hot water, but my nose and face were icy cold from being exposed to the freezing after-the-storm dry air.

"My Papa would have said if I'd a been a snake, I would'a bit you, Sleeping Beauty," she teased.

It took me a few seconds to get my wits about me before I sputtered, "Emma Cooper! What are you doing here? How did you find me here?" Of course, I already knew the answer. I had left a trail in the snow a New Yorker fresh off the stage could have followed blind-folded. Then, "Would you mind turning your eyes away so I can get up and get my clothes on?"

She laughed and covered her eyes with her hands in a sweeping theatrical motion. I scampered out of the pool and got dressed without looking back at her.

"I left Star of Midnight tied to a tree down where the mountainside levels out a bit," Emma told me between bites of bacon and fresh cornbread I had served her. She smiled and took a sip of hot tea.

"She's a fine horse," I said.

"Where did you get her?" Emma asked.

"She was happily browsing in some tall grass down the river from Alma," I said. "When I recognized her, I figured it was only right for me to bring her back to you."

"Where is Zeke?"

"Zeke? You don't need to worry about Zeke or anybody else coming down the pike claiming that horse doesn't belong to you."

"Is he dead, or is he still out there somewhere searching for me? What did you do to him, Jed?"

I held up both of my hands, palms out, and raised my right shoulder in a small shrug. "As God is my witness, Emma, I did not lay a finger on Zeke Jones. Just take my word for it you need not trouble yourself about him ever again."

She narrowed her eyes as she took in my answer, then went back to eating her breakfast. That was the last time the subject of Zeke Jones ever came up between us.

When she finished her tea, she set the mug down on the rocks by the fire, stood up and stretched, looking up at the mountaintops. "This is a beautiful place," she said. "We went to the hot springs in Arkansas one summer when I was little, but I don't remember the springs or the land being anything nearly as magical as this place. How did you find it?"

I shrugged and said, "I wander a lot."

"There is only one other place I have seen in this territory that catches my imagination like this place does," she said.

"Oh, where is that?"

"Do you know how the stage road comes up Kenosha Hill and you go through those flat woods on the top and suddenly the whole of South Park jumps up right into your face when you come out of the trees?"

"Yeah, I do," I said. "That sight is what told me that South Park and its surrounding mountains would be my home for the rest of my life. I never intend to go anywhere very far from here."

"It had the same effect on me," she said. "I told Dirk as we were driving down that pass that I would stay in these parts forever. He said he understood completely. He made a big show out of lining up my deal with Brett Smith for an exclusive one-winter engagement, but he did it just because he could get a higher price that way. He knows I'm not planning to leave as long as there is paying work to be had."

She turned and said, "I'm going down to check on Star. Don't you go anywhere until I get back, Buster."

I chuckled and said, "As far as I know, that trail is the only way out of here, so I can't go anywhere without you seeing me."

After about an hour, Emma came huffing back into our camp. She walked over to me without a word, took my hand, pulled me to my feet and led me over to the edge of the deepest hot pool.

Her gray eyes sparkled and she smiled. "That hot water is inviting. Help me out of my dress."

Well, she turned around with her back to me and started unlacing the front of her dress, high up near her neck where it was drawn tightly closed. Maybe she turned away to save me from embarrassment, because my mouth flapped open like a corral gate and blood rushed to my face as I stood there struck dumb and unable to move.

"The buttons, Jed," she said. "I can reach them by myself, but it will take half the morning."

So, I undid the buttons running down the back of her dress from the nape of her neck all the way down to the top of her hips. Emma reached up with both of her hands and pulled the pins out of her hair. She shook her head a little and her shining black mane cascaded down around her shoulders and back. She shrugged out of her sleeves and took care of removing the rest of her clothes on her own, before she turned to face me.

I believe I stated previously a lack of confidence in the existence of a God who takes an active interest in the continued workings of the world we live in. But, as I write these words today, I have to admit the balance of all of my experience tells me, with one pan of the scales weighed down by every evil act I have seen men do to each other and every disease and calamity I have seen befall the ones dearest to me and the apparent heavenly indifference to all such things, that this heavily-laden pan is far more than overbalanced by the other pan of the scales holding the simple sight of Emma Cooper standing there naked before me on that cold autumn day with white snow on the ground, warm mists rising from the hot springs, and a lone raven soaring in the blue sky above us. Any Creator with such an artist's eye is far more glorious than anything expounded upon by the preachers in their Sunday morning rantings or the Greek philosophers in their finest erudition. On that morning, I became a True Believer. The details of my personal theology have yet to fully emerge, and likely never will, but that singular memory is the only religion I need.

Emma Cooper helped me out of my clothes and led me into the pool. We cavorted in the hot water for a while, me splashing and making jokes to hide my embarrassment, then she swam over and kissed me full on the lips. She took my hand and led me to the smooth sandy edge of the lower end of the pool where the water spilled over and down the creek to the next pool. She lay back into the warm water and pulled me down beside her. We kissed and I caressed her silken skin for a few minutes before she quietly guided me inside her.

Being the young fool I was, it was less than three hours later as we descended the trail back to where Star of Midnight waited that I asked Emma Cooper to marry me. She smiled at me and shook her head. "Don't be ridiculous," she said. "What happened up there today was wonderful, but it is our secret. You know I am not one to settle down. Marriage to me would open the gates of Hell right onto your doorstep. I will meet you back here from time to time, but don't you ever bring up the idea of marriage again."

So, I didn't. I don't know what her motivations were that first time in the hot springs. I don't know if what she did was an act of unbridled passion, an expression of heretofore unrealized affection, or a simple payment for services rendered, but I do know what we shared over the next year must have been something like love. I know I have never felt those things again in the half-century since then, despite knowing many other women in the lonely days since Emma was taken from me.

Not long after Christmas in 1861, Death came calling on Buckskin Joe in the company of a ten-year-old girl named Rosarita Suarez, riding up from San Luis with her parents in an oxcart loaded with expertly tanned sheepskins and fresh-smoked mutton the family hoped to turn into cash to help see them through the winter. Pablo Suarez was well-known among the old-timers in the gold camps. His goods were always first-rate and worthy of the rather high prices he managed to negotiate for them. He was primarily a sheepherder, but he dipped his fingers into many different pies over the years, as did most people who lived in Colorado in those days.

Pablo had just made a deal at the General Store to leave two dozen sheepskins there on consignment when I greeted him out front on the porch. "Hola, Pablo!" I grinned and held out my hand to shake. We hadn't seen each other in about a year.

"Jed! It's good to see you, my friend," he replied in clear English with the precise Spanish accent I found musical and intriguing. I knew a little Spanish, but my American accent made it almost incomprehensible to a native speaker, so I didn't make much use of it. "Go in there and buy one of my sheepskins before they are all gone." He grinned as he said this, but I knew they would not last long, since winter was upon us and people loved having warm covers for their beds and chairs.

"How are Maria and Rosie these days?" I asked.

"They are good, . . . good!" he smiled and continued, "and they are here with me! Raphael Gonzalez offered to watch our place and take care of the animals so we could all come together on this journey."

"Wonderful!" I said, "I would love to see them." Little Rosie reminded me of my sister Evie, with her bright smile and enthusiasm for seeing new things and visiting with people and just enjoying life in general. Pablo and his family had taken me in for a few days at their little place outside San Luis when I had first gone down there on a trading trip, and I felt like family when I was with them.

"Can the three of you join me for supper this evening? I have a bean soup simmering that's almost as good as Maria's." Pablo nodded his assent and I pointed out my cabin on the slope at the end of town.

Emma joined us that evening and we enjoyed good company along with fresh cornbread dipped in my bean soup, which actually compared quite unfavorably to the savory dishes Maria had served me in her home. We laughed and talked and discussed the business possibilities we saw in the mining districts around the territory. Pablo had an eye for opportunities I was blind to, so I found our discussion stimulating. Rosie got bored with our conversation and curled up on some blankets and went to sleep soon after we finished eating.

I broke out a jug of Taos Lightning and poured drinks for the four of us who were still awake. We toasted our good fortune and the promise of the coming year. Even after the passing of more than fifty years, I still think of that toast and wonder if we didn't invite bad spirits into our lives that night by showing such unguarded optimism and confidence in our own power to determine our fates.

Rosie called out from her nest of blankets before we had put our glasses down, "Mama, estoy enferma."

Maria scooped her up into her lap and pressed her palm against her forehead. "Mi chiquita," she whispered, "you are burning up. Where are you hurting?"

The little girl reached around and touched her back. "I ache here," she said, "and all over, too."

I saw her feverish glassy eyes illuminated by the lantern flame and could see she was miserable. Emma got up and soaked a rag in the cold water in the bucket by the door. She knelt down beside Rosie and tried to soothe her with soft words as she wiped the cold cloth over her face. "Here," she said to Maria, "this might help her feel better. I will bring a pan of water over here where you can reach it." Then, looking at me with a concerned expression, she directed, "Jed, you should go find Doc Taylor."

I put on my coat and headed up the creekside trail into town. It was cold out that night, maybe the coldest night so far that winter, but there was not much snow on the ground. I stepped around the places I knew tended to be slick with ice and crossed Buckskin Creek across the little foot bridge that connected the two sides of town.

It was late evening, so I didn't bother stopping at Doc's office beside the general store or checking his rooms upstairs. He was a single man in his late thirties and a fine medical practitioner, but I knew he spent most of his evenings in the company of the dance-hall girls in the Buckskin Lodge and Saloon, either watching the shows or dancing or visiting the cribs out back. Tessie pointed me in that direction when I asked if she had seen him. I went out in the yard behind the saloon and called out just loudly enough for anyone in the long shed housing the cribs to hear, "Doc! Doc Taylor! We've got a sick little girl you need to see."

"Coming!" a voice from the darkness responded, accompanied by high-pitched feminine giggling. In a few minutes, Doc Taylor came out, hitching up his trousers as he stepped onto the frozen ground.

"I'll think she'll be fine," Doc said upon his first examination. "Probably a little touch of ague." I nodded my assent when he suggested we keep her in my cabin instead of in the cold bedding in the Suarez's camp at the edge of town. Emma and I fixed up places for the three of them to sleep on the floor near the stove, and then she crawled into my loft with me. I was a little embarrassed by her bold lack of decorum, but Pablo and Maria just grinned and wished us happy dreams. Of course, all we did up there was sleep—I'm not a complete social fool—with my arm resting on her hip and her cuddling against me while she snored lightly. And my memory is that I did have happy dreams, disturbed only by the times Emma climbed down out of the loft to check on Rosie and her parents.

Rosie seemed a little better around dawn, but then she couldn't keep her breakfast down and by mid-morning her fever was back up. By the time Doc Taylor came around in the afternoon, Rosie was delirious with fever and her face had broken out in small welts.

He looked her face over, poked and prodded her stomach and back and neck, then opened her palms and pushed up the sleeves of her dress to reveal more spots appearing on Rosie's hands and arms. He turned to those of us gathered in the room and said, "Smallpox. We need to close Buckskin

Joe down until this passes. Nobody in or out as of right now, especially not out."

He saw the fear and anguish in Pablo's and Maria's eyes and his manner softened a little. "I'm sorry," he said, "but in these cases with one so young there is little we can do but try to keep her comfortable. And pray, if there is a particular saint you pray to. That can't hurt."

Doc Taylor motioned me and Pablo outside to give us instructions about proceeding with the quarantine, then he asked Pablo, "Was there anyone sick in San Luis when you headed this way?"

Pablo nodded and said, "Raphael Gonzalez' wife was not well. She had been looking after Rosie and helping us load the skins onto the wagon the day we left. I remember she had a bad cough that morning. And, yes, Father Victor did not look good when we saw him the night before. But, that was almost two weeks ago."

"The timing would be just about right," Doc commented. "How are you and Maria feeling?"

"Good, . . . good," Pablo answered. "We are well."

But, by nightfall Pablo was in bed with a high fever and Maria was pretending to be just fine, even though her face turned pale and her eyes took on the same glassy sheen as Rosie's. The next morning, she was in bed and her face was breaking out in little pustules so close together that her skin resembled that of a reptile with evenly-spaced scales running up and down its body.

Our quarantine leaked like a sieve. As soon as the word "smallpox" left our lips and touched people's ears, the stampede began. Over the next two days the shopkeepers, lawyers and bankers, along with their wives and children if they had such, were nowhere to be found. Even the undertaker, a big brawny Irish fellow we all called "Moose" took off for Fairplay, declaring the ground was frozen solid and he couldn't dig new graves, so there was no reason for him to stick around. The people who stayed either had nowhere else to go, or they wanted to protect their claims from claim-jumping scoundrels, or in a few cases were decent souls like Doc Taylor and Emma who felt a duty to their friends and fellow townsfolk to help in any way possible.

A vigil began, with each of us doing what we could to make the Suarez family comfortable while we prepared our little town for a very long winter. Emma stayed in my cabin most of the time, cooling her patients' foreheads with cold, damp rags and bathing their bodies in cool water she brought in from the creek in buckets and poured into my tin washtub. Doc checked in a couple of times each day and made rounds up and down the creek looking for signs of new infections among the few remaining citizens. I cut and stacked firewood beside my cabin and then by Emma's place and then at three or four other places along the main road through town so people could take what they needed, if they ran low on fuel and were too sick to procure their own supply. Old Jim Riley gave me the keys to his store before he took off, and told me to let people have whatever they needed if their own supplies ran low. Tessie and some of the other girls went over to Moose's place and cleaned out the shed in the back yard so we could stack bodies, if such a need arose, until the ground thawed in the spring.

I know four or five people who thought they had special connections to God prayed, long and loud and with great emotion, in the little chapel out by the cemetery. A lot of us, less disposed to assurance about our relationship to the Almighty, myself included, prayed privately and fervently, hoping it would do some good.

On the twelfth day after little Rosarita took sick, Doc came down to the Lodge and announced the entire Suarez family was on the mend and he expected them to make full recoveries and be able to go home in a few weeks as their strength returned. Nobody else in town had fallen ill, so we all sighed with relief and many of us gazed heavenward and offered thanks.

The Buckskin Lodge and Saloon did a month's worth of business that night and stayed open until dawn. That night there was intense drinking and merriment and celebration among the good folk of Buckskin Joe, as we all thought we had dodged a big and nasty bullet. Near dawn, I noticed Doc Taylor sitting off by himself at a table in the shadows. His head rested on his arm, which encircled a half-empty whiskey bottle on the tabletop. I went over and nudged him.

"Doc," I said. "Maybe you should head home for a good sleep."

He roused himself and sat up straight. He glanced around the room at the lingering celebrants and said, "Life is short, my boy. Let us all celebrate the gifts we receive. And let me sleep here in this chair and enjoy my fellow citizens' happiness while it lasts."

It was only later that I remembered what Doc had said about "almost two weeks" being "about right."

By dark that day, Doc was in bed with a fever, aches, and chills that never let up. Three days later his face and body were covered with pus-filled sores and on the sixth night he died in his sleep. Seven miners and four dance-hall girls got sick in the same week, and thirteen more people were suffering in various stages of the disease by the middle of the week after that. Before it was all over, the shed out back of Moose's laying-out parlor was stacked with ten corpses which stayed frozen solid there in that dark little building shaded by tall spruce trees until the snow melted in late May and we could give them decent burials.

Throughout all of this, Emma never let up taking care of the sick. I think she sometimes went days without sleep, but I am not certain of that because I did not have the kind of stamina she did and often slept from dusk until well after dawn. Several of the men who stayed healthy formed a team with me to provide whatever Emma and the sick folks needed. We kept fires burning in their cabins, hot water boiling on their wood stoves, simple meals prepared whenever needed for anyone who was hungry, and we hauled the dead to Moose's, where some of the saloon girls prepared them for burial and sewed them up in shrouds before we took them out back.

One afternoon after we had carried water up from the creek to Tom Lilly's cabin, where Emma was looking after his brother, Tom took me aside and said, "That Silverheels girl is something special, ain't she? I've never seen anybody work so hard for so long in my life. She's made a real difference here. My guess is without her we would have twice as many dead bodies on our hands."

"Yeah, she is one of God's angels, for certain" I said.

Emma and I did not have a lot of time to ourselves during those days, but I did manage to go around to whatever cabin she was taking care of people in whenever I got the chance. I probably watched her more than was needed, keeping an eye out for any signs she might be getting sick. Since she was the one closest to the sick and dying, I worried for her, but I kept my thoughts to myself. As the days wore on, I started thinking those of us who were still healthy would stay that way. But, I saw that Emma was wearing herself down to nothing. I tried to talk her into resting more, eating more, and maybe even taking a few days by herself up in her own house. She refused every time, saying she was doing fine and did not need any advice from me.

During this time, Tessie was one of Emma's best helpers. She would take on the most unpleasant tasks without being asked and she had a kind and gentle way with the sick, especially the children, that is uncommon in anyone and unexpected in a saloon girl. During the rare quiet times, Emma and Tessie would sit somewhere and talk, and sometimes they would even sing together or break out in laughter. Emma took it hard when Tessie took sick, and I think it damn near killed her when Tessie died. She went into a somber mood any time one of her patients got sick enough for her to know they were not likely to survive. She wept a little when nobody was watching, any time one of them died. When Tessie went, Emma shrieked and cried out loud and wouldn't take comfort from anyone.

Finally, the sick either died or got well, and it appeared the epidemic had run its course. Emma consented to have me lay in a supply of food, water and firewood at her house, then she went home to rest, telling everyone she saw she would be fine and back at work at the Lodge before long.

That day the sky turned gray and light snow fell, coating the trees and road and hillsides with a fine layer of white. It had been a dry fall and winter up until that day, with a few small snows that had lingered a few days, then melted away everywhere except in the deepest shade of the biggest evergreen trees. But it had been unusually cold, and the present storm had not brought any warmer air with it.

I went to bed that night, tucked under a thick pile of blankets and furs up in my loft, with the cook-stove practically glowing red from the fire I stoked in it before I went up. I slept soundly, even though my hands and face almost went numb with the cold drafts creeping in through the log walls and between the joints in the roof.

"Jed, wake up!" A hot hand on my shoulder gently shook me into wakefulness. My loft was cold and no light came in around the window-shades.

"It's me, Jed. Emma."

"What? What's wrong."

"I want you to take me away from here tonight, before the snow gets deep. I want to go up to the hot springs. Get up. You have to help me."

I heard her feet reach the floor as she backed off the ladder, then I crawled out from under my warm coverings and followed her. I lit the lamp and adjusted the flame so it was not too bright, but bright enough to see her. She stood in the middle of the room, dressed from head to foot in warm winter clothes, with a large bag and bedroll slung over her shoulders. Her black hair spilled out from around a fur hat pulled tightly over her head and ears and her gray eyes beseeched me to get on with waking up and doing her bidding.

"Sit down, Emma. It's cold as Hell in here. Let me get the fire stirred back up and get some hot food ready while you tell me what's going on."

I went to the wood box and extracted a few sticks of kindling, then opened the firebox in the front of the stove and stirred the ashes back to life with the poker. I eased the kindling onto the glowing embers and blew softly across them until they danced into flame. Then I closed the firebox door and turned to face Emma.

"I'm getting sick, Jed," she started, then said, "I'm sick and I know I'm going to die."

"You can't know that," I protested, but she cut me short with her eyes.

"Just sit there and listen, Buster," she said, "this is the most important thing I have ever asked of you. I want to go up to the hot springs and I want to die up there, not down here among these people in this little town. This place is important to me, Jed. These people matter to me. I don't want them to know I am sick and I do not want them to see me when my face turns hideous like poor little Rosarita's and all the others' did."

I saw by the lamplight the moist glassy look in Emma's eyes I had seen in so many of my friends over the past month, the glassy look that said they were sliding into the darkest days of their lives. But, I think I lied to myself and thought it was just the cold and the dark that made her look like that. I could not imagine life without Emma, even though I figured she didn't feel the same way about me, so I refused to think the worst.

"Emma, you're just tired. You can't get sick. Remember you and me and the cholera out there on the prairie and how we didn't catch it? Besides, the whole town loves you, Emma," I said. "Even if you did get sick and your face turned ugly as sin, they would still love you no matter what you looked like."

"Maybe they would, Jed, but I would not love myself, and I can't stand the thought of that. I feel ugly on the inside, ugly and bruised, in ways you could never understand. My beauty and my singing are the only things I have to hold onto. My whole life, all I have wanted to do is sing and dance and entertain admiring crowds up on a big stage. Even if I live through having this God-cursed disease, I will never look the same. I will never be the great black-haired beauty everyone comes out to admire. I know I sing well, Jed, but it is my beauty they all pay to see. I won't have their memory of me scarred by the pockmarks on my face and arms and hands. Don't you see, Jed?"

I didn't see and I wasn't convinced she was sick or that she would die, but I went along with her plan, anyway. I packed the things necessary for a two-week absence and loaded them onto Fred's back, behind the saddle. Emma rode on Fred and I walked. The snow was coming down hard for most of the trek, and was deep enough that Fred and I were having some trouble slogging through it by the time we came to the steep chute leading up to the springs. Dawn was a couple of hours behind us, but the heavy clouds kept the scene dark and unsettling. I coaxed Fred to climb the steep rocks, with both of us slipping back a couple of feet for every three we went up, but we got Emma up there without any spills.

I helped Emma settle into the little stone spring hut and built a fire on the stone hearth to drive out the gloom and supplement the warmth rising from the hot water running beneath the floor. I unsaddled and unloaded Fred and led him into his stall, where a mountain of hay was stacked at his disposal. When I got back to the hut, Emma was fast asleep, curled up beneath blankets on the wooden plank bed platform. I gently felt her forehead. It was white-hot with fever. My blood ran cold and fear gripped my heart.

Over the next few days, her disease followed about the same course as the illnesses of the other citizens of Buckskin Joe. Back pain and muscle aches with relentless fever, then the appearance of the angry pus-filled dimpled spots on her face, which spread all over her body, even to the soles of her feet and the palms of her hands. She was mostly incoherent when she wasn't sleeping and muttered to herself like she was not aware I was sitting beside her. We had some good moments, though, when she seemed to get better for a while and could sit up and eat a little and carry on good conversation.

I tried to stay awake the whole time we were up there at the hot springs, but I have to confess I drifted off to sleep more and more often as the days went by. I did everything I could to keep Emma comfortable. I fed her when she would eat, soothed her hot face and neck with cool water, and wrapped blankets around her to stave off the chills. I watched her in her sleep and wished I could make her believe she would always mean the world to me, no matter what her face looked like after she got well.

"I don't want to be buried," she told me out of the blue one morning, as if we had been mutually discussing the relative advantages of differing funeral arrangements for some time.

"What?" I said, holding a cup of hot tea between my hands.

"Don't bury me," she said again. I thought she might be delirious again, but I looked closely at her and saw the old bright life shining in her eyes peering up at me from the bed covers.

"Don't talk about dying, Emma," I said. "You're really sick, but we saw some of the people in town recover after being much worse than you." I said this wishing it were true, but the fact is I knew that she was as sick as the sickest of them, especially the ones who didn't make it.

"You're wasting my time, Buster," she whispered through a weak smile. "I'm not going to last much longer and we both know it. I'm not going to be needing my body after I go, but I don't want to think of it lying under the cold ground slowly rotting away. You have to do this for me, Jed. Build a big funeral pyre like the ones I've read about in India. I want to be burned completely away so this horrid face will be no more and my soul will have nothing to worry about leaving behind. Scatter my ashes up on Kenosha Hill and around this place and around both of our houses. And don't say a word to another soul about it. Let them think what they want about me, that I ran off and didn't want to be seen again, or anything else you make up, but don't tell them what really happened to me."

I didn't say anything, thinking she would drift back into sleep if I stayed quiet. She closed her eyes for a moment, then they popped open wide and she said, "Promise me, Jed."

Seems like I spent a lot of my time back then figuring out how to keep promises to Emma Cooper.

"Okay," I said. "I promise."

She closed her eyes again and whispered, "You're special to me, Jedediah P. Carpenter. You know that, don't you?"

Then she drifted back into a deep sleep.

And she never woke up.

Fred and I worked for two solid days breaking through deep snow to find dead wood to carry back to the hot springs. I wanted to do the job right for Emma, so we cut and hauled wood until we had raised a pile ten feet across and four feet high, with a thick layer of loose tinder beneath a pile of kindling, then larger wood criss-crossed into a tight structure that rose to the top. I piled sticks of firewood into crude wooden steps so I could reach the center of the pyre to lay out a blanket, and then to lay out Emma's body on top of it. It was still snowing hard when I put her up there, so I covered her in another blanket, making sure her face was hidden as I am sure she would have requested, and I stood for a few moments watching the snow pile up on top of her where it soon created a soft sculpture showing the contours of her face, breasts, arms and legs in pure white.

I climbed down and lit the tinder, blowing softly into it until the flames spread sideways and upwards, consuming tinder and kindling in their path until the bigger pieces began to burn. Soon, I had to back away from the heat as the entire structure roiled in flames and smoke poured into the sky, swirling into a luminous dance with the falling snow. The boiling sweet-salty aroma of wood smoke and searing flesh on that gray winter afternoon is another memory that will never fade from my soul.

When the burning structure collapsed inward on itself, I did not utter any words to the Lord or incantations to any other spirits that might have been present that day. It was too late for any of them to intercede on Emma's behalf in this world, and I was certain she could take good care of herself along whatever path lay open to her in the hereafter.

All I did was whisper, "Goodbye, Emma," in a voice so low only I could hear it over the crackling of the flames and snow-blanketed stillness of the surrounding forest and mountains. Then I collapsed into the snow and wept. I wept for Emma and I wept for my baby sister Evie and for my dead parents and for all of my friends who had been taken so quickly that month in Buckskin Joe. Mostly, I think, I wept for myself.

I kept all of my promises to Emma.

The next spring I scattered ashes from the center of her funeral pyre, first on Kenosha Hill and then around our houses in Buckskin Joe, and finally back at the hot springs, spreading a little gray powder evenly around the pools and near the doorstep to the stone hut.

First, though, after the fire had burned cold and I had cried myself empty and slept like the dead until the following morning, Fred and I went back down to Buckskin Joe. Fred snorted and blew on the way down in a way he usually reserved for steep uphill work, and I wondered if he was not crying for Emma himself as he left deep mule-prints in the snow. We rounded the bend at the lower end of town and clumped through deep drifts up to the Lodge. I hitched Fred to the rail and went inside.

Brett Smith greeted me from behind the bar. "Hey, Jed, we were worried about you, wandering off in all that snow. Where have you been?"

"Just taking care of some business," I said. "It's good to be back. A little whiskey would go a long way towards warming me up."

He poured me a drink and asked me, "Do you have any idea where Silverheels is?"

"I don't have any idea," I said, being entirely honest in my answer since, theologically speaking, I was telling the whole truth.

"Some of the boys and me had a little meeting the day after she went up to her cabin to rest. We decided we needed to do something special for her to thank her for everything she did during the epidemic. So, we took up a collection around town and came up with five thousand dollars in gold and cash we want to give her."

My jaw dropped a little before I said, "That's damn generous. I'm sure she will be pleased." I reached into my vest pocket and pulled out Zeke Jones's gold pocket watch. "Here," I said, "add this to the pot."

Brett held up his hand to stop me. "Hold onto that for now, Jed. It's the strangest thing. Our little committee went around to Silverheels' place right after we took up the collection. It was snowing right hard by then, but we noticed there weren't any tracks leading away from her house. We knocked but got no answer. Old Jack Reynolds pushed her door open and called out to her, but nobody answered. He went inside and said her stove was still warm and her bed was all rumpled up, but there wasn't a living soul inside that house!"

"Well, that's real strange," I said. And I left it at that.

So, the committee waited until spring for Silverheels to turn up, but she never did. Some people said she really was an angel and she had ascended into heaven right there from inside her cabin, which would explain the lack of tracks in the snow. Others figured she couldn't stand the idea of being around the people she had seen so sick, or she couldn't stay where she had lost so many friends so quickly, and she had slipped away before the storm hit and caught the stage in Alma for points east or north or west or south or anywhere except for Buckskin Joe. None of them ever could explain why she left Star of Midnight behind at the livery stable.

After the snow melted in the spring and nobody had seen or heard from Emma, they gave the gold and cash back to the people who had contributed to the pot, at least as honestly as they could figure out how to do it. And, by general agreement, they started referring to the big mountain looking down from across the Platte as "Mount Silverheels" in her honor. Her story soon spread to Alma and Fairplay and beyond, and the name of the mountain stuck.

My narrative has reached a reasonable stopping place. When I started on this project back in December I figured to get what I wanted to say written down in just a few pages covering my entire life from my earliest memories to my doddering old age. I intended to tell about my years scouting for the First Colorado Cavalry Regiment, and about wandering in the southwestern deserts and the Grand Canyon. I might have described my few successes and my greater number of failures in various business enterprises since the boom went bust in Buckskin Joe. But, my fingers have been far more verbose the past few months than my tongue has been throughout the years and I am close to running out of paper and ink and patience for continuing on with this.

The snow is deeper now than I have ever seen it here in Buckskin Joe. It may be well into summer before the melt gets far enough along for people in wagons or motor cars to come back up here poking around for historic relics and other things to carry off like they've been doing with greater frequency the past few years. Somebody will probably come into my cabin here and poke around.

He or she might lift the floorboards and find this Last Will and Testament. That somebody must be you, you thieving scoundrel, since you are holding it in your hands and reading it.

That's all right, though. I have no need of these words or my belongings any more. A few minutes after I pen these final words, I will bundle up in my warmest winter clothes and strap on my snow-shoes one last time for the trek up to the hot springs. I hope my frail old lungs can get me there.

I expect that Emma is waiting.

The End

Historical Note

This story is fiction. It is based on the legend of Silverheels and some of the historical events surrounding the early years of the territory that became the state of Colorado.

Most of the people in this story are fictional, but some actually existed, including William Green Russell, Silas Soule, H.A.W. Tabor, Augusta Tabor, Baby Doe Tabor, the Reverend John Dyer, Buckskin Joe Higginbottom, and a dance-hall girl known as Silverheels. All dialogue in this story attributed to these historical figures is made up by me and should not be considered an accurate portrayal of the speech or thoughts of those individuals.

The written history of the early Colorado gold camps is imprecise and filled with gaps, maybe because the people in them were too busy to write their stories down. A notable exception is that of John Dyer, whose autobiography, *The Snow-Shoe Itinerant*, inspired some of the events fictionalized herein.

The real stories of Silverheels and Buckskin Joe Higginbottom are obscured by the mists of time, but their existence as real people can be inferred by the geographic features named in their honor by their contemporaries.

The Mosquito Hot Springs are my own creation, although similar hot springs do exist throughout the Rocky Mountains.

-John Erwin, December 3, 2012

"Into the Snow" is available in paperback, ebook, and audiobook formats. For ordering information or for general comments, you can contact me at johnerwin60@gmail.com. I answer all non-spam messages, but be patient in case I am temporarily somewhere out of the reach of the internet. -JE

Made in the USA
Lexington, KY
12 November 2019

56900065R00105